Praise for *Rooting Interest*

"Even a real-life WNBA game can't compare to the high-stakes drama of this gorgeously rendered, thrillingly queer journalist-meets-athlete romance."

—Emma Specter, *Vogue* culture writer
and author of *More, Please*

"Whether or not you're a sports fan, you'll cheer on Felix and Natalie, two women figuring out what they want in life. *Rooting Interest* is smart, nuanced, and desperately sexy."

—Amy Spalding, bestselling author of
For Her Consideration and *On Her Terms*

Rooting Interest

CAT DISABATO

831 STORIES

831 Stories

An imprint of Authors Equity
1123 Broadway, Suite 1008
New York, New York 10010

Cover design by C47
Book design by Scribe Inc.

This is a work of fiction. Names, characters, places and incidents either are products of the author's imagination or are used fictitiously.

Print ISBN 9798893311037
Ebook ISBN 9798893311044

Printed in the United States of America
First printing

www.831stories.com
www.authorsequity.com

For Zan

You know what you did

1

Stepping into the arena, I feel a familiar crackle. The air sizzles like it's charged with electricity, like in the moments before a thunderstorm breaks.

The final few minutes before a game begins is my favorite thing about sports. It doesn't matter if the setting is a barely groomed field in a hidden corner of a suburb or a brand-new, state-of-the-art, $200 million facility in a major city. The feeling is always the same: anticipation, suspense, but most of all, possibility. Any team could come out on top. Any player could have the night of their life. The goals are specific and simple: play well; win. Off the field it isn't so simple, but that hardly matters here. Nothing gets me down in these moments. No matter how far I've drifted off course.

I'm supposed to be on the familiar sidelines of an NFL practice field, developing a rapport with Los Angeles Cougars rookies and coaxing quotes out of the coaching staff. While the guys ready their bodies and their plays during training camp, I am supposed to be filing stories about the new football season for the *LA Chronicle*. Instead, that beat—*my* beat, the one I fought for through innumerable late nights and with ruthless competence—has been plucked out of my grasp, as if it'd never really been mine at all.

For reasons too painful to consider closely—namely, that I am the sports section's only queer female staff writer—my editor reassigned me to cover WNBA All-Star weekend in Phoenix. I'm here because of my repeated requests to write more features, my editor, David, insisted, but the features I'd been pitching him were about football. Imagine my surprise when the response to my pitch about the Cougars' offensive weaknesses was an assignment to cover Natalie Czapski, the star player for the Hollywood Lights, and her comeback after an ACL injury.

I've never written about basketball. I've hardly ever watched it. But now, a scant few hours after booking my travel and scrambling to make my flight, I am going to have to figure it out. Even if the ground beneath my feet feels no more solid than sand.

At least the energy in the PHX Arena is familiar, the excitement sparking the air, boosting my mood and calming my anxiety as I wind my way through the crowd. Fans who look like they've been following their team for decades mix with overstimulated kids, couples holding hands, and chattering groups of friends. All-Star weekend means people are decked out like the color spectrum: red for the Las Vegas Aces, seafoam for New York Liberty, and burgundy for the Lights. In my usual work outfit of a black button-down and black pants, I fade into the background, just as intended.

I try hard not to come off as anyone or anything in particular when I'm on the job. To ticket holders, the press badge around my neck means I'm someone official, and to players, I'm nothing outside of my game knowledge and the questions I ask them—more of a conduit than a person. It's something I learned from David, who was David Greenebaum, sportswriting legend, before he was my mentor and my first-name-basis boss. Now that I am unexpectedly in a position of having to win back a job that I thought was mine, following David's lead—playing by his rules—is more crucial than ever.

When I make my way to press row, I'm mildly surprised to discover that it's right behind the announcers' table, close enough that I'll probably hear their commentary. I find my assigned seat between a young Black guy, who gives me a tight smile with "no new friends" energy, and a white person with a dyed-pink mohawk and, helpfully, a "they/them" pronouns pin.

They look at my badge, then my face, then my badge again. "Wow, is the *LA Chronicle* finally covering the WNBA? Or is this just for Nat's comeback?"

The small placard in front of them identifies them as a freelancer, someone used to being batted around by whatever publication decides to say yes to a pitch. And they clearly know that covering women's sports is still seen as optional at most big outlets.

I know how to play this. I shrug and say, "I go wherever they tell me to go."

They stick out their hand. "Danny."

"Jennifer Felix," I say, shaking it. "But everybody calls me Felix."

As I busy myself plugging my computer into the power strip taped to the table, Danny makes conversation. "It'll be good to have CZ back in the four spot."

It's like they're speaking in a foreign language that I studied in high school, some vocabulary familiar but the full extent of the meaning lost on me.

"Totally," I say.

"Or do you think she'd do better in the five?" Danny asks mildly.

"She's, um, I think she's got something to prove so she'll step up in any role." It's not like I've said anything wrong. The problem is, I haven't said anything at all. When sportswriters talk, we argue about minutiae and one-up each other with niche facts and hot takes. I can tell from Danny's raised eyebrow that they can see right through me, see how little I know.

"Oh, honey," Danny says, almost sympathetically, but with a vicious little edge. I wonder suddenly if they'd pitched a WNBA story to the *Chronicle*, gotten the feedback that there wasn't an audience, only now to see someone totally ignorant of the game plopped down next to them to cover it. "You're really fucked, aren't you." Not a question.

"I'm a fast learner," I say.

"You better be," they say, and pointedly turn back to their computer. Conversation over.

I'm rattled, and I know it shows. Determined to shake it off, I return to my setup, straighten my laptop, and shut down any application I don't need. Sports is a world full of rituals (or superstitions, to the nonbelievers); players have their lucky socks or listen to the same song before every tip-off. And I have mine. I close my eyes. I take deep breaths through my nose. I listen to the sounds of the crowd, note the scents in the arena. The voices aren't just energized; they're giddy, and much more high-pitched and femme than what I'm used to from NFL fans. I hear the squeak of rubber soles on the arena floor and heels on the stairs. I smell popcorn, ketchup, and Dove deodorant.

This cataloging is a practice I copied from David. He wrote a book called, simply, *Writing the Game*, which my father gave me for my sixteenth birthday. My copy is so dog-eared, underlined, and just generally run-through that it's falling apart at the binding. One of the lines I've committed to memory: "Attending a sports game as a fan is a five-pronged sensory experience, so writing about sports should be the same." One twisted bra strap digging into the skin of my shoulder is the last sensation I identify before opening my eyes. I slip my hand under my shirt and untwist it, making sure everything is in its right place. I'm as ready as I can be.

The announcer's voice booms, *"Welcome to All-Star weekend!"*

The screams of the crowd swell to a new crescendo as the announcer starts calling out the first few players, none of whose names I recognize. Cameras flash as the announcer rumbles, *"Back from a season-ending injury to show us what a Big can do in this competition, and representing the Hollywood Lights, it's CZ, Natalie Czapski!"*

In my rush to research three decades of WNBA history, I'd reduced Natalie to her component parts: her wingspan, her layup, the design of her Nike sneakers, the muscle she'd put on after her rookie year and the speed it gives her. In doing so, I somehow failed to understand what Natalie looked like as a whole. She glides onto the court, all long-limbed grace. Her blond hair is pulled into tight French braids. On the Jumbotron, I can see how the turquoise blue accents on the Lights' uniform bring out the richness in her pale eyes. And how her big, crooked smile, which stretches across her whole face, makes her seem a little cocky—but also kinetic enough to power the sun. The way the tip of her tongue pokes out slyly between her teeth makes something hum in my rib cage.

She flexes her right bicep and laughs when the crowd goes even wilder. There's no way for me to hear her, but I can read her lips as she screams at them—at us: "LET'S FUCKING GO." My stomach and chest pulse with little bursts of want. Fuck. In my rush to get ready for this new assignment, I'd somehow forgotten that the WNBA is filled with my exact type: pretty tomboys with bravado. I'm pummeled by the unprofessional thought *Natalie Czapski is hot!!* I *never* had this problem in the NFL.

I can't afford distractions right now, so I turn my attention back to my notes. Tonight's the skills competition, followed by the three-point shooting contest, and I watch the first three players blaze through the stations, writing down their times for their exercises (39.2 seconds, 45.1 seconds, and an unfortunate 55.6 seconds).

I log any game vernacular that isn't immediately familiar to me in a section of my doc called "Terms and Lingo." For the Cougars, I have meticulously organized research and notes and quotes, everything at my fingertips and ready for me to draw on in an instant when inspiration either strikes or lacks so much that I need to rely on previously accumulated information. My new file has a "Questions" section that is twice as long as the rest of the document, filled with inquiries that I'm sure are mind-numbingly basic to even casual fans. Things like "What does it mean to 'space the floor'?" and "Where did Natalie Czapski go to high school?"

As I type, fast without looking at the screen, I watch Natalie in her seat, her infectious smile only disappearing when her jaw drops in awe as a contestant lands a neat three-pointer. Scanning the crowd, I see I'm in good company: Natalie's getting attention from all over the arena, everyone from former teammates who playfully squeeze her shoulder as they pass to a brunette sitting courtside in a handmade "CZ DOES IT" T-shirt. She is a magnet, drawing in focus and metabolizing it into charm.

When it's her turn, she strips off her warm-up jacket, springs on the balls of her feet, and shakes out her elegantly muscular arms. At the whistle, she's off like a rocket. This is when my years of sportswriting—even about an entirely different game—pay off. Some highly trained sliver of my brain automatically translates what she's doing on the court into dynamic language. She bounces passes into a row of progressively smaller nets, hitting her mark on the first try for each. She races toward the basket, sets up at the initial shoot zone, and drops her ball cleanly through the net. As she sinks the next, I note the way her fingertips graze the ball and the flex of her calves as she jumps with her shot. She's stunning to watch.

Natalie finishes her run with an easy layup and plants her hands on her thighs, her chest heaving with deep breaths as the announcer's voice booms out her impressive time: *28.2 seconds*. From the vibe of the arena, I can tell that no matter how the rest of the night goes for Natalie Czapski, she's shown everyone that she is *so* back.

She wins the skills competition—it isn't even close—and I take note of reporters buzzing around me. "That footwork—never would have known anything had ever been wrong with her knee," a guy with a buzz cut says. She could've stopped there and relaxed into the loose, playful atmosphere of All-Star weekend, but instead she goes into the three-point contest radiating the determination of someone with something to prove.

A player named Ruthie Jones makes enough three-point shots that it feels like no one can beat her, so when Natalie starts shooting, the crowd is loud and yammering, not paying much attention. But Natalie is doing even better than Ruthie, making more baskets than she's missing. The whole mass of us goes holding-our-breath quiet, falling into that calm that swoops in during a big play when it feels like an errant shout could disrupt the equilibrium and throw a player off.

"No," someone behind me whispers in awe. "She literally can't do it."

I glance back at the fan, two rows above and wearing

a Czapski jersey; the Lights' logo, a playful riff on the Hollywood Walk of Fame stars, is nearly glowing on her shirt. The fan is squeezing her friend's hand, eyes locked to the court and sparkling. "She can't, she can't, she can't," the woman chants, but she's breathless in anticipation, using the negative to invoke the opposite: *She can, she can, she can.*

Next to me, Danny murmurs their own writing out loud, a copyediting trick to catch errors. "No player has ever won both the skills competition and three-point contest in the same WNBA All-Star weekend."

Natalie isn't just doing well; she might be setting a record. My own fingers fly over the keyboard as my eyes stay glued on her. She grabs her last ball, bends her knees, and shoots. It arcs balletically and slips cleanly through the basket. Even I know enough about this sport to think the word *swish.* The reverent hush gives way to explosive cheers. Natalie Czapski has made history.

I feel a flutter in my chest, the way I do when an article goes viral, like maybe this is less of a demotion than I thought. I could write a great piece here, especially if I trust that my storytelling skills are just as valuable as being a ball-knower. My uncertainty gives way to a more familiar feeling: determination. There is a good story to tell about Natalie, and I'm going to figure out how to tell it.

As I flash my badge to the security guy at the door of the media room, I hope I'm radiating "Can you believe this night?" buzz and not anxious "I'm new here" energy, but the feelings are a little muddled.

Basketball might be uncharted for me, but the organized chaos of this presser—press conference—is not. I'm intimately acquainted with the symphony of scuttling PR women backed by the frenetic clack of fingers on keyboards, the chaotic disarray of tangled laptop chargers and extension cords, broadcast camera people setting up their gear elbow to elbow. My eyes bounce off the smattering of old white dudes—they are everywhere in sports media, as pervasive as crabgrass—and slow to scan the faces that make me feel an unexpected sense of belonging. Even though I don't recognize anyone in the room, there is a surprising sense of the familiar in the people around me: a woman with a taper fade haircut, someone holding a laptop with "Protect trans kids" stickers, and a guy in the corner with a fully beat face. I can picture these people out at the dyke nights I go to in LA—just not at my sports bars. But here they are, with barely suppressed excitement to cover what turned out to be a momentous athletic event.

I find my seat in the second row. I start my voice recording and hope it doesn't catch my audible intake of breath when Natalie is ushered into the room. She was alluring from across the court. From less than six feet away, she's spellbinding.

I pull up the gamer on my laptop screen, the recap article that I need to publish as soon as possible, and while I review my stats and check the spelling of players' names, the reporters around me start asking questions.

"Natalie, congratulations. How does it feel to make history tonight?"

Like most professional athletes, she's been media trained into oblivion, giving the kind of basic, boring responses that allow beat writers to file their pieces and her to avoid controversy. It's standard stuff, nothing really inspiring. Tracking the patterns in the questions themselves is more interesting. We are supposed to be celebrating, but after that first question, everyone seems to have already moved past the significance of the moment on to the future of her game, asking about the pressure she faces, soliciting comments on how much is riding on her. I imagine my fellow reporters typing phrases like "crushing weight," "grim intensity," "tall hill to climb." I've made it as far as I have in my career by pushing into a story as far as it will give, and I sense there's something else we aren't getting here, something to be gleaned from that ever-present smile.

Natalie's night wasn't about proving something in the wake of her injury, I'm realizing as I take her in. It was about the joy of playing the game. This is a narrative I can weave without knowing all that much about basketball; I just need a good quote from her to make the piece work.

"We have time for one more," the team publicist says, and my hand shoots in the air faster than anyone else's.

"There, on the left."

"Hi, Jennifer Felix, *LA Chronicle*," I respond, pushing aside the flicker of warmth pooling in my stomach when Natalie turns her attention to me. "You looked like you were having a lot of fun out there. Were you having fun?"

"Yeah, I was having a great time out there. Anytime I get to be on a basketball court and playing, I'm happy."

Anytime I get to be on a basketball court and playing, I'm happy. It's a good kicker. I nod. "Thank you!" I respond.

Natalie's smile drops, and with a jolt I realize she doesn't see what I'm after. And that the version of her that radiates brightness has a darker flip side, a stone wall that blocks out the light.

"That's it?" Her voice is teasing, but not breezy. There is a real bite in her tone. "That's your question? Did you really just ask me if I *enjoy* playing basketball?"

"I wanted to hear about how you felt on the court tonight," I answer uneasily, the warmth in my core replaced by a sinking feeling.

"Do you have a basketball question? Because I have some basketball things to talk about." She rests her elbows on the table and leans forward, homing in on me.

Watching this on playback, a casual observer probably wouldn't read anything into our exchange because of Natalie's careful tone. They wouldn't be able to see the way Natalie's eyes lock on mine and the fact that there's no give in them, no humor at all. Her stare is a razor-edged challenge, a test I know I'm going to fail. I can't ask a basketball question because it will reveal that I don't know what I'm talking about, but if I don't ask a basketball question . . . it will also reveal that I don't know what I'm talking about.

"That's it from me," I say, hoping she'll let it die.

She doesn't.

She leans back in her chair, folds her arms across her chest. “I haven’t seen you before. Do you know the league?”

I want to tell her that watching her play made me more emotional—felt more visceral—than a sporting event has in years. But that’s not something a journalist can say, so instead I give her four words that couldn’t be more passionless: “I’m working on it.”

Her eyes narrow. “Working on it,” she parrots, pushing back her chair. “Well, thanks for trying, I guess. Goodnight, everybody.” Then she walks out of the room, never looking back. I watch her go, shock giving way to anxiety and then painful, red-hot embarrassment.

II

I file my gamer in a daze, get a car back to my hotel, and turn to my second-most-effective coping mechanism: blasting AC/DC while trying to recite, from memory, any random football player's stat line. To shake off Natalie Czapski humiliating me personally and professionally, I make my way through Travis Kelce's yards-received from every year of his career, in order. In 2014 it was 864—no, 862. In 2015, it was 875.

Though I can't stop a thick rope of embarrassment from knotting itself under my breast bone, I manage to effectively blot out any real thoughts, at least until I make it back to my room at the Marriott. I tug the AirPods out of my ears, and the "Thunderstruck" guitar lick becomes a faint and tinny echo. Alone, unwitnessed, I can't help but realize how scared I am that no matter how hard I work, how expertly I follow the rules and meet the expectations others set for me, I won't get to have the life I want.

I fight tears, because I'm incapable of crying just a little bit. Hyperventilating sobs and snot all over my face will only make me feel worse. And once I start, I can't stop. So instead of letting myself, I rip one of the thick hotel pillows off the bed and scream into it until my eyes stop stinging.

I strip off my bra, sigh in relief, and toss it somewhere near the window, then dig through my suitcase, throwing aside work clothes until I find a big T-shirt and my softest sweats. After all that, I finally get to activate my first-most-effective coping mechanism: FaceTiming my best friends.

Casey joins the video call first, with Sean half a second behind her. Just like me, their backdrops are a hotel's bland furniture and taupe wallpaper. But unlike me, they are in familiar hotels, where they always stay when they're on their usual beats. The disparity of our situations threatens to crack me back open, even as their usual greetings—Casey's "Heyyyy girl!" and Sean's "How are you?"—comfort me to my core.

The three of us were hired within six months of one another, after a bunch of old-timers took a buyout and the *Chronicle* tried to make their sportswriting "younger, hipper, and more relevant." By luck, we fit together like puzzle pieces: Sean, just as stats-obsessed as me, with an encyclopedic memory of NBA history; and Casey, a collegiate soccer star whose career ended on a knee injury, who then channeled all that frustrated potential into becoming an agnostic sports obsessive, with photography and video-editing skills to boot. Casey writes about everything and produces all the sports social media content for the paper. The *Chronicle* is wasting Sean's potential as the third guy covering the Lakers and the Clippers, and he spends every waking moment trying to break out. We're all overachievers, as competitive and intense as the athletes we cover.

"I saw Czapski did good tonight," Casey says, just as Sean asks, "How is it going over there?"

I slump onto the mattress, covering my face with one hand while holding up the phone with the other. I recount the nightmare presser, and they gasp and groan in all the right places.

"Fuck her! That's rude as shit," Casey says, sipping on a Modelo while glancing away from the phone screen, presumably toward her TV, where she's probably streaming at least four different games at the same time. She'll watch whatever happens to be on at any given moment, from Formula 1 to golf to the Little League World Series. I don't take her split attention personally; Casey always has one eye on a match.

Then there's Sean, who stares at me through the screen with an almost off-putting level of eye contact. "This situation is not a reflection of your skill or talent or dedication," he says. "You're an incredible writer who has been put in an impossible situation, and just because Natalie *fucking* Czapski doesn't know that doesn't refute those facts."

I wish I shared Sean's easy, matter-of-fact confidence in me, but my own self-assessment is more confused. Some days I feel like the best writer that's ever been in print, and some days I feel like a talentless hack who has gotten to where I am by force of will alone.

"Hear, hear," Casey says, tilting her beer bottle toward the camera, content to let the most emotionally intelligent member of our trio take the lead on comforting me. "This piddly bullshit is *not* going to break you."

Sean raises his drink—some craft IPA poured into a tulip-shaped glass—and sips as well.

The tangle of anxiety in my chest finally starts to fray and loosen.

An alert pops up on my screen: an email from David.

I say my thankful goodbyes to Sean and Casey, but as soon as I open David's message, my brief respite turns to churning dread: Given Natalie's performance at the skills competition and the above-average number of clicks my write-up is already getting, David wants to step up our coverage. My assignment for the next day has been changed from a piece on Natalie's comeback to a full-fledged profile of her as both a player and a personality.

Which means now I am going to have to spend an entire day following around someone who has already called me out and write something I'm proud of—something that impresses David enough to give me more opportunities, ideally in the league I actually know.

Do you have a basketball question? Well, I sure as shit am going to have to come up with some now. I drag my laptop under the covers, shoving three of the pillows behind my back so I can lean comfortably against the headboard.

I text Sean, "If I needed to learn how to write about basketball overnight, where would I start?"

Sean sends me an article from *Defector* literally titled "How to Watch Basketball" and then, seconds later, a piece he wrote about the Lights last year, right after Natalie got her injury. An hour later, we hop on Zoom and start watching one of the team's games from last season when Natalie was still playing. Sean points out her strengths, her weaknesses, and the little things you can see when you've been tracking a player for their whole career.

"I really, really appreciate you," I say after the game's final buzzer sounds.

Sean shrugs, very *aw shucks*. "I can't let the *Chronicle* get a reputation for running schlocky stories about basketball," he says, but it sounds like "I've got you."

"I love you too," I say, and close my computer and then my eyes.

III

Normally, I hate it when a publicist shadows my interviews—it's a deflating reminder that my subjects are putting on a show for me, and that any candid-seeming glances behind the mask are likely carefully planned, or at least previously vetted. But today, when I have to tail Natalie Czapski for hours, I'm grateful for the buffer. There's so much about her I'm desperate to ignore. My low-level attraction to her, a persistent hum, queasily mixes with the reminders of last night—both my terrible performance and Natalie deliberately embarrassing me. I'd prefer anything to being left alone with her—and it seems the feeling is mutual.

When we all meet up in the players' hotel lobby, Natalie doesn't say hi. She just gives me a nod that communicates "I'm here because I'm required to be" and turns back to her phone.

Our minder, Ashley, picks up on the rancid vibe and glances anxiously between us like she's watching a high-stakes tennis match.

Nobody is happy to be here. But also, it's to my benefit

to smooth things over. If Natalie wants to make me feel unwelcome, good luck; I cut my teeth as a young woman writing about American football. When David assigned me to the Cougars beat, the resounding response by the sports journalist community was either "Her?" or "Aren't women supposed to be sideline reporters, not beat writers?"

Also: I date women in Los Angeles. Cool, hot LA lesbians are scary. In both my professional life and my personal one, I've been training to deal with this particular cold shoulder for as long as she's been practicing free throws.

Ashley introduces me to Natalie as "Jennifer," and I take it as an opportunity. "Call me Felix," I say with forced positivity. Natalie glances up from her screen, and I catch her eye and quirk my mouth into what I hope is a friendly, sly smirk. "No one needs another dyke named Jen."

Natalie snorts, a helpless gasp of almost-laughter and a smile she can't control. The joke was a desperate attempt to gain favor with Natalie, to show her that even though I don't know her game, we at least play for the same team. She immediately schools her face back into a bored blank canvas and looks back to her texts, but it was enough. A little crack in her shell.

Ashley clears her throat. "The car's here," she says with the tone of a passenger on the sinking *Titanic* who just spotted a rescue boat. As Natalie falls into step beside her and I trail behind them, I realize Ashley probably heard "dyke" as a slur rather than a reappropriated affirmation. Or maybe Ashley isn't so much scandalized as surprised—it could be that she just didn't clock me as gay. I try not to look visibly queer when I'm on the job, in part because of the conservative bent of the sport I typically cover and in part because I don't want to look visibly *anything*. I want to be as nondescript as possible. I want people focusing on my questions, not considering how I'll receive their answers.

When I'm working, I keep my hair down—thick, wavy, and black. I wear black trousers and silky button-downs, which I buy one size too big and then cinch with a black leather belt. It's an outfit that can do a million things. If I'm forced to be on camera, I can throw on red lipstick and look striking but professional. If I go out to a queer bar after work, I can unbutton my shirt a little too low and pull my hair up into a slick bun that shows off my undercut. And most importantly, when I wear it as is, it doesn't look like anything at all. The players don't think a single thought about my appearance.

Natalie's day—and thus, my day—is jam-packed, starting with a short ride in a chauffeured black SUV to our first event. During our five-minute drive, I try to get a conversation going.

"Last night was a big night. How are you feeling this morning?" I ask.

It's a soft, open-ended question, designed to give her the space to say basically whatever she wants. I always start out this way with players I've never interviewed before. On some level, athletes are performers, and performers love to put on a show; all you have to do is give them a stage. *If you build it, they will come.* This has been true my entire career—except, of course, with Natalie *fucking* Czapski.

"I'm feeling great," Natalie says, without looking up from her phone, where she appears to be responding to a group chat. "Fun weekend."

I imagine the rest of my day, hours trapped with someone saying as few words as possible with barely disguised disdain. As frustrating as it is, a sick little thrill starts to build inside me.

I hate being out of my depth in public, my inadequacies revealed in front of an audience of my peers—but I love a private challenge. Whenever my friends' necklaces get tangled, they bring them to me. Hand me a cracked coconut, and I'll pry it open with my bare hands to get at the liquid inside. I start to consider my strategy for finding chinks in her armor.

When we get to our first stop, a brand brunch, servers are passing around trays of mimosas and mini fry breads, offering Glossier-pink napkins with their free hands. Some enterprising catering chef has found a way to make bite-sized chilaquiles.

Natalie breaks away almost immediately, practically sprinting across the room to embrace a tall Black woman in her late thirties, a pretty stud with short, tight dreads. I'm left alone with Ashley, who seems to have intuited my lack of experience and is prepared to fill in the gaps—perhaps to make up for Natalie's chilliness. "That's Louisa Bozley, Nat's best friend." She juts her chin toward the duo. "They both went to Iowa State. Weesie was a big help with Nat's transition to the W."

Weesie = Louisa, I jot down in my Notes app. Nicknames

are a big enough thing in the W that in less than twenty-four hours, I've heard Natalie referred to as "Nat," "CZ," "Natty," "Big Natty," "Natalie the Natural," "The Natural," "Big Natural," and, when she shoots threes, "Natty Ice." In my post-video-call late-night cram session, I watched an interview where another player referred to her as "The Smooth Operator herself."

"We're not going to get her back until brunch is over," Ashley says, putting away her phone in the pocket of her blazer and turning to actually look at me. "Off the record, she hates doing media, avoids it as much as possible, and only really agrees when it's good for her teammates or for the W. Anything to help grow the league."

Ashley is older than me, in her late thirties maybe. How long has she been working to get people to pay attention to this organization? How often has she endured someone who doesn't know the league coming in to write about it? How often has *Natalie* been interviewed by a journalist who has zero knowledge, little interest, and a fast-approaching deadline?

This time, my pang of embarrassment lacks the defensiveness from the night before. I tell myself a story about Natalie, about her constantly answering questions from reporters who don't care enough to follow women's sports before writing about them. Though the W has exploded in popularity over the last few years, Natalie's been playing long enough to remember the era of indifference. I realize my arms are crossed, and I drop them to my sides. I decide to forgive Natalie her prickliness, her defensiveness in the face of yet another journalist who barged into her world, knowing nothing but somehow empowered to shape the narrative.

I'm good at figuring out what people need and giving it to them. Natalie needs someone who is as competent and knowledgeable on the page as she is on the court. I can't be that for her right now, but I can use this time to get closer.

I survey the room, stuffed to the gills with current and former players, people who work for the league and their handlers, and see this morning for what it is: an all-access pass to their world.

"I'd love to chat with some people for background on the league and Natalie's career," I tell Ashley, with as much specificity as I can muster.

"Great." Ashley nods. "Who do you want to talk to?"

"Everybody."

For the next hour and a half, she leads me around the room. I meet two of Natalie's Hollywood Lights teammates and their coach. Last year's WNBA MVP stops on her way to the bathroom to say, "Natty is *that bitch*, and you can print that, that's on the record." A columnist from *The Athletic* takes pity on my inexperience and catches me up on the rivalry between two of the other players on the Lights, one of the big storylines for the season—can they put their warring aside to play great ball together? I absorb lingo at a breakneck speed, taking notes like "the stripe = free throw line" and "illegal screen, you CANNOT MOVE." In between interviews, I snatch canapés off passing trays and guzzle champagne flutes full of mocktails.

It's like basketball speed dating, the whirlwind of new personalities and new information, and I'm exhilarated. In my impotent frustration with being reassigned and the subsequent embarrassment, I didn't have space to focus on the excitement of splitting open a new world filled with rich history and stirring storylines. The joy that creeps in is a combination of my love of sports and the thrill of doing my job well, of knowing I can bend the world to my will if I try hard enough. Without seeing myself, I know my cheeks are flushed.

Ashley returns to my side, and I point across the room at a high femme Black woman with thick fake eyelashes and very short, blood-red nails, who looks a little on the short side for a basketball player but keeps pulling other players into tight, affectionate hugs. "Who is that?"

"Allison Altman. She just retired; she used to play for the Aces."

"Can we chat with her?"

"Um, actually . . ." Ashley's eyes swing across the room and land on Louisa Bozley, who is standing near one of the bars. "Let's go speak with Weesie—she can give you some great insights into Natalie's game."

Louisa beckons Ashley over as we approach, and then we're off to the races.

"Natalie takes these shots from the three, and a lot of defensive players can get flustered when they shoot threes, but she is so smooth." Louisa has the voice of a Shakespearean actor and speaks with the same passion. I feel something kindred between us: the type of person who can watch an incredible player and see art. It's not fair that they call soccer "the beautiful game" when all games are so stunning in their own right.

"Was she always good with a three-point shot, or did she have to work at it?" I ask.

"You've presented me with a false dichotomy here, and I think you know it"—Louisa raises her brows at me, and I laugh—"but if forced to choose between two extremes, I'd say Natalie knows how to work rather than resting on the laurels of baseline talent."

As I jot down this quote, I already see the shape of a story forming: The pairing of raw talent and relentless practice, which operate like interlocking gears that make an athlete perform like she does. What happens when injury grinds those gears to a halt. What it takes to set them back in motion.

A few minutes later, Ashley hustles Natalie and, by extension, me back into our SUV. I follow Natalie into the big back seat and, taking advantage of our proximity, I launch right in. "I spoke with Louisa Bozley about how smooth you are when you take your three-point shots. How did you hone that?"

Natalie actually looks at me, for the first time all day. "That sounded dangerously close to a real basketball question."

"I'm dangerously close to a real sports reporter," I say.

"And if I ever needed to talk to somebody about the Cougars, you'd be the first person I'd call." A dig, but less sharp than I might have expected. A dig from someone who's taken the time to Google me. Like the almost-laugh from my dyke joke, I'll take what I can get.

"Okay then. If I were a real Lights reporter, what would I ask you about the shot?" The driver takes a sharp turn, and I grip the door tightly to avoid knocking into Natalie. Even so, I sway into her space.

"No, it's just like . . ." Natalie blinks at me as the car rights itself, and I shift away from her. She looks up at the ceiling, out the window, and then back at me, considering her answer before responding. "I have worked a lot on my three—focused on it. The three shot is just going to get more important. I want to be a three-and-D player my team can rely on. I want to be the future of the game."

Helpfully, "three-and-D" had come up with Sean—as he put it, "It's gotta be someone with the coordination and the stamina to be both an offensive and a defensive weapon."

"Well," I say, jotting down notes on my phone. "If your performance last night is any indication, you're well on your way."

"Let's see how I do in a real game." Natalie's dismissive, but she flashes me a proud little smile, and it somehow feels even more powerful than her big smiles do.

IV

The day is well-choreographed: a volunteer outing at a kids' camp, a closed-door meeting with the players' union, a photoshoot for Skims where I dutifully take notes on what it means that not *only* the whitest, straightest, and femmest athletes have been cast in the campaign. I don't write down the other things that can't escape my attention: the cut of Natalie's hamstring muscles arcing out from underneath her shorts, or her husky laughter in response to something another player, Cameron, whispers in her ear.

Before that evening's All-Star festivities, Natalie changes into an alarmingly sexy look—black suit pants and a jacket hanging open, no shirt underneath—to head to the arena. In the car on the drive there, she answers my questions just as she's done all day, but with all that extra skin on display. I can't help but stare from the side of the "orange carpet" as a line of photographers shout her name and then from the outskirts of a cocktail event in one of the VIP lounges. Then, suddenly, Ashley is escorting us into our seats, one row up from courtside. Natalie is on one side of me, and Ashley is on the other, but with the rush of energy in the venue and the proximity of the action, Ashley is as ignorable as an airplane seatmate. For the first time all day, I feel very nearly alone with Natalie.

We watch in silence as the All-Star game begins, the mood friendly and low-stakes. I wonder how she feels not being out there, how much it hurts to be on the ascent but not back on top. The starters take showy three-point shots over the heads of purposefully languid defenders. Though technically there are teams, and winners and losers, tonight is more like a victory parade that happens to take place on a court.

Looking around the arena, I can't help comparing the crowd with what I'm accustomed to at NFL games. There are plenty of women and queers and people of color who love to watch football, but here, I'm surrounded by hot lesbian couples and their adorable children, elder queers who've probably been season ticket holders for almost as long as I've been alive, multigenerational families wearing the WNBA's Black Lives Matter shirts from the 2020 season. I know the WNBA isn't some magical fairyland where bigotry and hate don't exist, but here, it's like the volume on it is turned down.

Natalie chats with a redhead on her right, who she cordially—if coolly—introduces to me as the girlfriend of one of her teammates. When the woman gets up to go to the bathroom, I take it as an opening. "And how about you? Do you have a girlfriend?"

It's the kind of question I'd ask any player I was profiling, but I also can't pretend I don't remember Natalie's hand on Cameron's hip during the photoshoot.

"Nah." Natalie's voice is syrupy. "I'm married to basketball." A beat. "And I'd never cheat on my wife."

I snort. It's a good line, one I'm sure she's used before. Still, it's definitely going in the piece.

"So . . ." I seize the flicker of warmth between us. "What happened with your ACL tear?"

Natalie looks momentarily stricken before she controls her face, dropping any expression at all in favor of generic calm. I can't quite make sense of her reaction. She must be used to fielding questions about it, and frankly about little else in the last year.

"What do you mean?" She asks blandly, and her absence of emotion catches my attention like a flashing neon sign. She's tucking something away from me. She's a jar with the lid stuck tight.

"How did it happen? What were you feeling in the moment?"

In the dozens, if not hundreds, of times she's answered that line of inquiry, she's probably given more or less the same response she gives me now: "Just lost my footing," followed by a shrug.

I need to break through, and I have to do it quickly. Without thinking too hard about what exactly I'm doing and why, I mentally shift from my reporter mindset toward something more akin to how I act on a first date, when I'm hungry for quick intimacy and I want to cut out any bullshit game playing.

"So, as I think you've guessed, I've never written about

basketball before." I watch her face for clues on how to proceed.

She looks startled, thrown by another change in topic. "I don't have to guess. There's this thing called Google. You can look up journalists and see what they've written about."

There's snark in her voice, but unlike at the press conference, I don't have to shut up.

"Let's have a conversation off the record," I say.

Natalie raises an eyebrow and nods.

"I'm pretty sure my editor only assigned me because I'm the one queer woman on the sportswriting staff," I say, a little more quietly. Natalie's eyebrows go higher. I maintain eye contact.

"This assignment sucks . . . for both of us." I'm deciding how much to share on the fly, but I try not to sound hesitant. "This assignment sucks for me because I was taken off a beat I spent a long time fighting to get. And it's unfair to you, and the Lights, and the whole league that they didn't at least put a basketball writer on this."

Natalie looks like she doesn't know what to say. Sharing this much—anything at all about myself, really—this almost never happens between players and journalists.

I nod, like I'm giving myself the signal to continue. "But I'm a really good writer, and I'm willing to put in the work. You have a right to be pissed at the paper for not covering women's sports properly and you even have a right to be mad at me, but if you keep stonewalling me, my story won't be as good, and that won't help either of us."

She leans closer to me so she can speak lower. "This shouldn't be my responsibility."

"It shouldn't be." I nod emphatically. "But this is where we are right now, and I'm choosing to embarrass myself in front of you by being honest if it helps me write a better piece."

Around us, the crowd roars. In unison, our eyes flick back to the court, the game, then back to each other.

She sighs, loudly enough that I can hear it through the cheers. "What do you need from me?"

"I need you to tell me about last season. The injury, what it meant for you and the Lights, and the recovery. Tell me something about it that you haven't given to every other journalist who's asked."

Natalie gives me a scowl, and somehow it's almost as pretty as her smile. Maybe because our petulance feels mutual; it finally feels like we're in this together.

"I'm really fucking tired of talking about it, and of giving some bullshit answer about what was—how did you put it?—'going through my head at the time.'"

Your answer doesn't have to be bullshit, I don't say. We're not there yet. "It won't be the whole article, I promise," I tell her instead. "And if you talk to me about it once, we won't talk about it again. Asked and answered."

Natalie turns her gaze to the court, thinking, and her eyes are away from me for long enough that I look over too and watch Sabrina Ionescu sink a three, then smash her chest happily against Caitlin Clark's.

"All right," she says lightly, as if we aren't having a breakthrough. As if she isn't really conceding anything.

"We're going back on the record," I say.

Natalie nods.

"Take me through that moment, when your injury happened."

"You've never played anything, right?" she asks, instead of answering me.

"I thought we were really going to talk about this?" I don't attempt to keep the annoyance out of my voice.

"I'm getting to it, I promise." She smiles big. She smiles like she knows what her smiles do.

I roll my eyes. "I played Little League and hated it, and youth soccer and hated it."

She laughs. "How did someone who hates sports get your job?"

I shrug, giving her my own version of a big smile: no teeth—like a cat who's swallowed a canary, I've been told. "I never said I hate *sports*. I just don't like playing them. I like to watch."

She laughs, from her chest, like it's actually funny instead of a joke on the level of "that's what she said." It's not my comedic chops that she's responding to, I know. It's that, finally, we're loose.

"Okay, so it's hard to explain to someone who has never played, but time can be different on the court. It can get really slow or speed up, or you lose track of it. I've talked to a lot of players who got injured, and they all say that when they got injured, time sped up so fast that they barely remember it happening. But for me, it was like I was on super-slow-mo, every second stretched out."

It turns out, when Natalie relaxes, she's a talker. I don't dare interrupt, typing notes into my phone with furious speed as Natalie explains how she heard her tendon pop before she felt any pain, how she told the trainer who helped her off the court that she'd be playing again by the fourth quarter even though she knew deep down she was done for the rest of the season. The frustration of watching from the sidelines. The way PT was somehow the hardest thing she'd ever had to make her body do. And how happy she was to step back onto the court for the skills competition. "I thought I was going to feel rusty out there, but it was the exact opposite. It was like my body didn't know how to miss."

Natalie's lips curve into her small, more private smile again. In it, I can see all the raw, unfiltered pride she's trying to gulp down.

But then she shakes her head, as if to snap herself out of it, and when the grin drops from her face, I see a flicker of something sharper underneath. "Was that a good enough story for you? Asked and answered?"

I can tell she's holding something back, and though it's not as if I expect players to tell me everything, I'm somehow disappointed. Her answer was somehow both more emotionally honest than anything I've heard from an athlete in a long time and also more artfully deceptive, designed to conceal some other, deeper truth.

I want to pick at it, to prod her forward, but instead, I say, "Yeah, that was great," and hope I'm a better liar than Natalie Czapski is.

A little after midnight, I file my story with a suggested headline, "Natalie Czapski Doesn't Know How to Miss." It's a good piece, with a great narrative arc and the kind of sensory detail David loves. "At its core, all of sportswriting is about either the thrill of victory or the agony of defeat." It's something he'd written in his book and frequently repeated in the newsroom. This profile of Natalie has a little bit of both. Now I just have to hope it's enough, not only to get me back on my NFL beat, but also to make him seriously consider my feature pitches.

I arch backward over the hotel desk chair, relishing the cracks in my spine and the stretch in my shoulders, which are always tight after spending hours with my fingers on a keyboard. I'm wired from the work. On a normal game day, I'd run a blisteringly hot bath and soak until the heat leeched all the energy out of me. But tonight I have another option: an after-party.

I dig through my suitcase looking for an outfit that somehow communicates both "I'm a professional who belongs in this room" and "I'm a really fucking hot person who belongs in this room." I stick to my usual black trousers but opt for a silky black tank top, so thin it's nearly translucent. I pull my thick black hair up into a bun, revealing my undercut. If there's anything I've learned over the last twenty-four hours, it's that there's no real downside to appearing queer-coded in this space. I know that the combination of black hair and green eyes gives me a striking, alien-like quality that can draw people in, and riding off the high of filing this story, I'm buoyant at the thought of it.

But on my way to the players' hotel, I have a flash of panic. *Am I loosening my own reins too much? Revealing too much of myself?* Even though I'm going to a party, I am on the job, that in-betweeny nature of an event that can be called a "work thing." It's a professional-ish setting, and I've never had to consider who I am, personally, in those. I pull the tie out of my hair, letting the thick waves cover my undercut.

When I give my name and step into the banquet room, my unease evaporates. The lights are low, and the crowd is rowdy. I can hear laughter and enthusiastic conversation over the City Girls blasting from the speakers. *Of course I want to be looked at here*, I tell myself. But I keep my hair down.

I make my way over to the bar, order the old-fashioned that's been calling my name, and find an empty spot against a back wall to take in my drink and the scene. After a few minutes of cataloging the people in the room I can identify and those I can't, I feel someone slide up on my left. Natalie Czapski—still in her black suit with no shirt. My breath catches in my throat.

It's part of my job to mask my feelings, to sit

expressionless in the press box when my favorite quarterback makes a beautiful touchdown pass and the crowd erupts with joy all around me. I've had to work through exhaustion, hunger, a full bladder—but on the job, I've never had to sublimate desire. I will my heart to stop stuttering.

Natalie says something to me, but I can't hear her low voice over the music.

"What?" I shout.

She shifts closer to me, and her mouth creeps so dangerously close to the side of my face that I can feel her lips moving when she says, "You aren't bored and lonely back here, all alone?"

She turns her head so I can respond, and I'm close enough to catch her scent, fresh and floral, petrichor and jasmine, like Los Angeles after it rains.

"No," I say into the whorl of her ear. It is decked out with a row of silver hoops and is small for her size, and something about that makes me feel tender. "You already know, I don't mind watching."

She laughs, low in her throat. Our faces switch positions again, Natalie bent over me. "It wasn't as bad as I thought it was going to be." Her voice is thick and warm, and I realize she's drunk. Not too far gone, but far enough past tipsy for everything in her to have eased. "My coach says I need to really marinate in anything before I really get it, but I get it now."

"What do you get?" I ask in her ear.

"It was good to finally talk about my injury—cathartic,"

she says, lips close but talking more crisply, like she's making sure I hear every word. "You're not going to fuck me over, are you?"

I shake my head hard, emphatic.

And then suddenly, I feel Natalie's fingers brush the nape of my neck. She lifts my hair, revealing a bit of my undercut.

"Look at you," she breathes into my ear.

I feel a pulse of want and an intense urge to touch her back. I sputter out a breath.

A group of players comes over, and one tugs on Natalie's arm and shouts something in her direction, jarring us out of the moment. Natalie pulls her arm away from me, and my hair falls back into place. I ache at the loss of closeness. Natalie smiles and nods at her friends, then starts to follow them toward the other side of the room. Before I'm out of earshot, she turns back quickly and says loudly over the music, "See you later, Jen!" She laughs manically, like she's just shared the funniest joke she's ever heard. And I grin because that joke was mine.

As I make my way back to the bar for another old-fashioned, I wipe away my smile and set my jaw. Once I have a drink in hand, I find an even more shadowed place to stand. Sipping my drink, I let my gaze drift over the crowd, resting on Natalie here and there but taking care not to follow her too closely with my eyes, as much as I want to. I might not know the feeling of being attracted to someone I'm writing about, but I have learned the hard way what happens when I fixate on a tomboy femme type who says things like "I don't do relationships" then slides her palms along my waist.

By the time I finish my second drink, the adrenaline has seeped out of my body, and on the way back to my hotel, I picture myself falling asleep the moment my head hits the pillow. Instead, I spend what feels like hours begging my brain to shut off and my body to calm down while echoes of the hot feeling of Natalie's attention buzz away relentlessly on my skin.

V

I know the article is a hit because while I'm on my way to the airport, Casey sends me a Natalie Czapski fan edit from TikTok, with a caption that references the line from my piece: "It's like her body doesn't know how to miss." I feel the aftershock of her hands on me at the after-party and swipe the video away quickly; the last thing I need is to train my algorithm to send me sexy footage of Natalie. Even though my WNBA assignment is over, wallowing in my attraction to a player is still ill-advised, even if it is a little refreshing to feel the zing of a crush—especially if it's maybe a little bit reciprocated.

After I clear security at the Phoenix airport, I get a Slack message from David: "Great work on the profile, Felix." I bloom at the praise. My own parents are workaholics, loving but distracted, who have given me a lot of nonspecific praise for things they don't quite understand my whole life. David is harder to please and knows the exact contours of a job, my job, well done.

On the quick flight home, I buy Wi-Fi service to masochistically read the coverage from my Cougars replacement—the pieces are fine, but notably absent are the storylines I've been setting up during the offseason. It's particularly frustrating to see most of the coverage focusing on the veteran players when the Cougars have one of the most exciting newcomers in the league, rookie Kyland Green, perhaps the most talented quarterback to step onto the field in the last decade. Not to mention, he's one of a very, very small cohort of Black men to play his position. Racism runs deep in the sport, enough that it's somehow still rare to see a Black man as a quarterback. He should be all anyone is talking about when they're talking about the Cougars right now.

As I debate sending a response to David asking when I should plan to head back to training camp, an email comes in from Ashley. When I open it and find a lengthy missive, I brace myself. Publicists only email after stories are published with a quick, perfunctory thanks or a request for a correction that typically takes the form of a scolding or a tantrum. So I'm not expecting what follows: "It's not often new reporters really understand the spirit of the league, and it was really a pleasure to see how well you captured it."

I grip my phone more tightly. It's not as if I'm unused to positive feedback, exactly. I have great relationships with the Cougars' PR team, and sometimes the players text me when they like my pieces. But something about this feels different, more personal.

"I don't think it will come as a surprise that I've read profiles from writers that are better at talking about the X's and O's of the game," Ashley's email continues. "But your story was the best I've read when it comes to capturing Natalie's style as a player, her particular blend of talent and hard work, her devotion to the game, and the joy she gets from playing. What makes her her."

Ashley's closing lines: "Natalie asked me to tell you that she also enjoyed the piece. She specifically said, 'Please make sure to thank Jen for me.'"

It would read as a nothing comment to anyone who wasn't in the room with us last night. The soft place under my ribs flares with warmth, without my permission.

I log into the *Chronicle*'s employee backend to check the analytics, and I'm shocked that the article is the second-most-read sports story of the day, only a few thousand views below a Dodgers gamer.

I take a screenshot and send it to my group chat with Casey and Sean.

"Our girl is cooking!!" Casey texts back.

"Hell yeah!" Sean replies.

Casey messages me separately, asking if I can record a video for the *Chronicle*'s socials to promote the story, and I bristle with frustration. I hate being the subject instead of safely behind the scenes.

"Please don't make me," I type back. "Can I do a voice-over instead? Maybe over a compilation of Natalie shooting threes?"

Casey sends an eye-roll emoji, then: "Fine. But for the record, I think it's a bad fucking move to run from the camera when you have a big story. You can't hide when people start looking for you."

I don't respond. I move back to the group chat. As much as I begrudge being thrown into All-Star weekend like I was, I have to admit, at least to myself, that it unlocked something in me to have to learn a new world, one that has different priorities. One that attracts unbridled joy, queer women, Black sisterhood. It's an environment that helped me tell a good story.

Below the screenshot of the great stats on my piece, I message, "I'm forced to conclude I'm a good writer."

"I'm forced to conclude people like sports regardless of the gender of the players," Casey responds.

"I'm forced to conclude that basketball is fun," Sean adds.

Focusing on the NFL and dedicating all my time and brain space to football had felt strategically sound, but maybe broadening my perspective would do me some good professionally. Editors like writers whose pieces do numbers.

"It's almost as if," I text, "Casey was right that watching other sports could make me a better football writer." I hope she'll take this as an apology for not responding to her other texts.

"It's almost as if," she responds, "I'm screenshotting this and will be reminding you of it every time you ever doubt me again." We're having two conversations at once, and I know my olive branch has been accepted.

Oblivious to the subtext, Sean replies, "Live in the good side."

This is Sean's personal mantra, and Casey and I have

adopted it. Things going badly? Can't change them? Find the good side and live in it, like choosing to walk on the sunny side of the street.

"Live in the good side," I respond. "Thank you both for joining me for this teachable moment."

"It's clear there's an appetite for deeper coverage of the Lights," David says in our one-on-one meeting on Monday morning. "So I'm going to reassign you to the beat full time."

It's like I can feel my blood coming to a boil. I've already missed four days of Cougars training camp, and every day I'm away I slip further behind.

"You should put a basketball writer on it." I frustratedly pick at the seam of one of the books lining the walls of David's narrow office that has a view of an unattractive bend in the 405.

This is as close as I've ever come to talking back to David, and he is so unaccustomed to me being surly that he doesn't read my tone properly, taking my exasperated rebuttal as an attempt at a helpful suggestion.

"I would put Sean on it if I could." He cleans the lenses of his glasses.

"Sean would be great," I press. It's actually the perfect solution. Sean and I have talked at length about how he won't be able to progress in his own career if he doesn't get his own beat. And he actually knows basketball.

"We need Sean to keep supporting Greg on the Lakers and Donnie on the Clippers—postseason coverage is doing too well for us to pull back." He's organizing stacks of newspapers on his desk now, not completely distracted, but not fully focused on our conversation either. "Plus, you're a great fit for the assignment."

I bristle, then I force my shoulders to relax down my back. I actively decide to assume he's referring to the quality of my gamer and the popularity of my profile. In the three years since he's hired me, David has always treated me like any other reporter, not like a female reporter or a queer one. I can give him the benefit of the doubt here.

"You're really hitting a stride with these pieces, and I don't have many writers I trust to pick up a new beat as quickly as I know you can. I need you for this." He pats the pile of papers in front of him with a smile, and his approval feels so gratifying, all my instincts scream that I should just do whatever he asks me to do, whatever he needs me to do.

"The next Lights game isn't for a week." He nods. "Your only job between now and then is to meet their staff and watch basketball games."

And with that, I'm dismissed.

VI

Back at my desk, in the buzzy scrum of the newsroom, I give myself a moment to recover. I try to swallow the sting of disregard and disappointment. I close my eyes, put my earbuds in, steady my breathing, and hit play. An observer would probably assume I've finally taken advantage of the free meditation app membership that our billionaire owner got every staff member as a holiday present last year. But no: AC/DC, again. I mentally recite the yards-passed stat for every starting QB from last year's NFL season until my chest unclenches and my rational brain comes back online.

Live in the good side.

My career might be skidding down a side road, but I've been given a gift that beat writers rarely get: time to research. And I absolutely fucking *love* research.

I smear off my lipstick with the side of my hand—the lipstick I wear when I want to "look professional" and "be taken seriously" but always take off as soon as it's no longer useful. I selfishly reserve the meeting room that all the sports and entertainment writers like best, the one with the biggest TV and no windows.

I lock myself inside this sanctuary, and for the next five hours I sink into women's basketball. I watch last year's final game, a commanding win by the Minnesota Lynx, then I queue up one from three years ago when Natalie scored her first triple-double. I Google "What is a 'screen' in basketball?" ("A screen, also called a pick, is an offensive tactic where a player stands in front of a defender to block or impede their path, creating space for a teammate to move freely.") I Google "best screens WNBA" and then watch until I understand both the science and the art of the pick-and-roll. I listen to the ESPN play-by-play commentator Ryan Ruocco say things like "Look at Czapski, just carving out space underneath the rim," and shout, "Natty Ice! You bet!" when Natalie hits a three.

I take a break to microwave leftover pad Thai and shore up my nerves, then turn on the game where Natalie tore her ACL. It's only six minutes into playtime, and it happens so fast that at first it looks like almost nothing. Natalie is moving forward, running through what I now know is called an open lane to the basket. She trips, she falls, she puts one hand on her left knee. The analysts don't even pause their banter. But they go quiet when one of Natalie's teammates helps her up and she tries to put weight on her leg, only to crumple back to the floor, her mouth open wide with a shout. There's no audio of the noise she makes, but I know what agony looks like on a player's face.

The commentary starts up again as Natalie's fall replays in slow motion. "Looks like Natty just lost her footing," says the female broadcaster, sounding surprised. Her use of

Natalie's nickname is fond and familiar, like she's forgotten where she is and is speaking out of concern for a friend. "She's in a lot of pain."

On the floor, Natalie's head tips back, her face illuminated by the arena lights, and I can see the moment she breaks. She cries. Not just a few tears that escape her eyes out of anguish but streams of them, like she already sees her fate. About five seconds later, Natalie's teammates—and one member of the Las Vegas Aces—swoop in and surround Natalie, holding up towels to block the view from the crowds and the cameras. But those five seconds are enough for me to understand. She's crying because she knows—in her gut, in her bones, in her ligaments—that her body is failing her. She's crying at the loss of her ability to play. My food tastes sour, and I push the plate away.

Two Lights staff members pick up Natalie and carry her off the court. The game restarts, and I watch the Lights battle valiantly but ultimately unsuccessfully against the Aces. Sometime during the second quarter, the commentator chimes in with an update: Natalie will sit out for the rest of the game. And that's it, they don't mention her again. I dig through the *Chronicle*'s WNBA archives and find nothing. I search online and see a piece in *The Athletic*, reporting on the nature of Natalie's injury and its impact on the rest of her team's season: "As for the Lights, they have lost a crucial part of their franchise rebuild. Hollywood has missed the playoffs the past three seasons, and Coach Branson previously claimed that Czapski's league-leading defensive abilities would be 'the most important factor in reaching the playoffs this year.' A season-ending injury for Czapski makes the Lights' road to the playoffs longer and harder." I already know the way the story ends; the Lights didn't make the postseason last year.

As if to distance myself from that game, I relinquish my hold on the good conference room. Back at my desk, I read everything the *Chronicle* has published on the W in the last ten years while the sun sinks low and the LA sky turns pink and orange. I take notes and absorb as much as I can, but as my eyes trace over a paragraph for a third time, I realize that I'm too distracted to absorb anything else. I'm thinking instead of Natalie's face. The look on it just before she started crying, when she realized her season was over. The joy spread across her features when I watched her on the court. And I'm thinking of the tug of Natalie's desire—of her hand as it slid onto my neck. A question? A promise? An offer? I wanted what she made me feel—seen, chosen, special. If I'd felt free to do so, I would've taken anything she offered me.

VII

My basketball deep dive continues over the next week. I attend practices, held in a dingy UCLA gym that clearly hasn't been updated since the 1950s and was probably rejected by every collegiate team on campus. It smells like old sweat covered by chemical disinfectant, and it's always at least five degrees too hot—the team doesn't run the ancient AC because it's too loud to hear plays called during scrimmages. On a rare stormy day, the Lights have to reschedule practice to accommodate marching band rehearsal, because the space doubles as their rain-day location.

"The owners are debuting a new practice facility next year," Ashley says, with a warmth in her eyes that looks like victory. She often sidles up to me on the risers for a few minutes, updating me on team happenings that could bolster my reporting. I like to think chatting with her gives me extra cover to watch Natalie sweat as she runs drills and leaps acrobatically to knock shots out of her opponents' hands.

Ten days after my first WNBA event, I drive to Crypto.com Arena—home of the Hollywood Lights, even though it's technically in downtown LA, not

Hollywood—and watch Natalie and the hotshot rookie point guard, Jada Jackson, buoy the Lights into a win against the equally ranked Dallas Wings.

In the media appearance after the game, Ashley calls on me, and I say, automatically, "Jennifer Felix, *LA Chronicle*." Natalie responds, "Hey Jen," nearly whispering into her mic like she's making an ASMR video. Heat pools in my belly, and I'm glad I've had years to perfect my poker face.

"I'm just playin'. Everybody, call her Felix." Natalie flicks one of her braids over her shoulder.

"Thanks for that, Natalie." I try to sound flip to convince everyone, myself included, that I'm keeping it together like the professional I absolutely am. I clear my throat. "After a few lead changes in the first half, the Lights stayed up all through the third and fourth quarters. We have all your stats—field-goal shooting percentages, number of defensive stops—but what did you guys see out there that isn't in the numbers? What are the intangibles?"

Jada's eyes light up. "Oooh." She glances at Natalie. "Weesie's off-ball action?"

Natalie nods, and they tag team to explain how Louisa's court awareness and the moves she made when she didn't have the ball helped create open shots for the rest of the team.

On Sunday, the Lights lose badly to the Connecticut Sun, and the vibe at the presser is notably less convivial.

"Hey, Felix," Natalie says, exhausted, when I raise my hand.

I choose my words carefully. "You were down more than twenty at halftime and never got within ten points of the Sun."

Natalie winces.

"How do you play through tough challenges?" Our eyes lock, and I try to convey an apology—or at least empathy—with my gaze.

"In a game like this one, you've gotta stop thinking about the score and the win and your record and the playoffs, and just start playing possession to possession." Natalie nods to herself. "I think, 'How can I make sure that on every possession, my team members get a great look at the basket?' Sometimes that'll bring you back for a win, and sometimes it just gets you through the game."

I reframe my entire gamer off the quote, reworking the lede and drawing out a thread about metabolizing failure, taking the opportunities as they come. As I file the piece, I know it's something I would highlight and underline and save if I encountered it while reading the paper. In making this WNBA assignment work, I'm playing possession to possession, and I'm also playing the game as it unfolds in front of me.

I puff up with the kind of quiet pride I think Natalie would recognize when David accepts my suggested headline: "Sometimes the Lights Just Have to Get Through the Game."

On Tuesday, the Lights aren't playing, but there's a big matchup between the Aces and the Sun. I grab a six-pack on my long commute from the office in El Segundo back to Echo Park, planning to watch the game from home.

My big one-bedroom on Sunset Boulevard has its pros and cons: I'm above a coffee shop / bookstore and a vegan restaurant and within walking distance from most of the best bars in the city. But I don't have a parking spot, and the bookstore hosts a bad monthly comedy night that I can hear clearly in my apartment. My air-conditioning is better than at the Lights' practice space, but it only really cools my living room. Thankfully, that's where I pass most of my time, curled up on a deep, plush couch I spent nearly a month's rent on, in front of the most important thing I own: A sixty-five-inch TV with the motion blur turned off.

I sit cross-legged on the sofa, pull a pillow into my lap, and settle in to watch the game, post my thoughts on social media, and go back and forth with other sportswriters who are doing the same, just like I'd do during a night off during NFL season. The balance I have to strike is hard, acknowledging that I'm new to both the W and basketball, but sharing the kind of information that will allow me to be seen as an authority. I fall back on describing the Sun's performance against the Aces in contrast with how they just played against the Lights.

At the start of the third quarter, a Sun bench player named Olivia Agwuegbo comes into the game and immediately starts heating up. Every time she touches the ball, she finds the space to attempt threes and mid-court shots. I check the *Chronicle*'s stats resource, then post to Bluesky,

"Agwuegbo is shooting at 78% from the field, her best performance since joining the WNBA six years ago."

Five minutes later, I get a text from "Maybe: Natalie Czapski."

My breath catches in my throat, and my thumb hovers over the alert without tapping on it. I don't know what Natalie is going to say, good or bad or strange, or if it's even really Natalie at all, and I want to live for a few moments in the place where everything is possible and nothing is defined. I wait until the message alert disappears and I have to open my phone to read the text.

"She shot even better in college," the message says.

Another one comes in as I'm reading. "Like, her field-goal average was 58% her junior year, that's crazy."

"Then idk, she lost it a little when she got to the W."

My brain's first response is instinctually journalistic: double-check Natalie's stats, then post a follow-up on Bluesky. My hands are back to my computer before I pause, my fingers above the keyboard, to fully process that Natalie Czapski just texted me. No—Natalie just texted me a response to a Bluesky post I published five minutes ago, meaning she's possibly, probably been reading my feed during this entire game. Maybe since before tonight.

I press my hands to my cheeks to confirm they're as hot as I suspect they are. My palm catches the corner of what I'm sure is a dopey smile. My body is responding like a high schooler's whose crush said hi to them in the hallway.

Luckily, it's easy to fake composure over text. "Thanks, I really appreciate it," I type back.

Then I fact-check Natalie's stat, confirm she's spot-on, and post a follow-up.

I open my messages again. "How did you get my number?" I toss off the question before I can overthink it.

"Ashley," she replies.

That's unusual. I'm in direct contact with a lot of NFL players as sources, but never has the conduit been a publicist. Maybe the procedures are different in the WNBA, and I'm about to ask her when another text pops up.

"You must be pissed, right? That you're not back to writing about the NFL?"

It feels like a test. I'm positive it's a test.

It's unfair, but I hate that our dynamic is flipped. She is supposed to be the one answering questions, not me.

I itch to reply quickly, with something noncommittal or a denial. But I force myself to slow down. I watch Agwuegbo sink a logo three to close out the quarter, and the studio cuts to the stands where her wife is sobbing from elation. This might be a run-of-the-mill game for the Sun, but for Olivia and her family, it's the biggest professional victory to date. It's one of the things I love best about sports—how on any given day something totally unexpected and magical and beautiful can erupt from someone's body. At any moment, something really fucking good can happen.

I pick up my phone. The last time I connected with Natalie, during All-Star weekend, she listened to me because I was being open with her. She likes honesty, and maybe she likes quick intimacy. Maybe that's what she trusts.

"It stings," I type. "Mostly because my editor wouldn't have reassigned me if I wasn't a woman, and that really fucking sucks."

I pause, my thumb hovering over the send button. I'd been thinking it from the beginning, that I had been given the WNBA assignment not because of my expertise as a writer but because I was a queer woman, but I hadn't ever put it so bluntly. I hadn't allowed myself to connect all the dots directly to David before. David, who I respect more than anyone else in this field, who I desperately want to respect *me* in turn—it was him, specifically, who had thought something like, *Felix is a queer woman. I should put her on this story.* David is the one who had made the facts of my biography more important than my expertise as a journalist.

I delete the message, and the heat on my face is different now. I'm not ready to share something so raw with Natalie, even abstractly. I try again: "A little pissed, yeah. But turns out I like watching basketball, and I like researching something new."

I hit send, and then I keep going. "And I love how gay everybody is." Send. "Even the straight girls." Send.

It's a lot of texts in a row, and I put my phone screen-down for a few minutes to save face. A player on the Aces gets a foul called on her, and she yells a little at a ref until her teammates circle around her and pull her away. "The girlies are fighting . . ." someone on Bluesky posts.

When I pick up my phone, there are new texts from Natalie.

"Sorry I gave you so much shit at first."

Then: "I can tell you don't have historical knowledge, but you're not saying anything stupid."

"I strive every day not to be stupid," I text back.

Natalie reacts "Haha," and I wonder if that will be it, but then the typing dots pop up.

"I strive every day not to be slow on the court."

"I strive every day to gain historical knowledge about women's basketball." My dopey smile is back.

"Text me when you have questions."

As I save her number, I consider setting her contact under one of her many nicknames but opt for Natalie. Just Natalie.

VIII

The Las Vegas strip has the wacky, unnerving quality of *Alice in Wonderland*. A roller coaster bisects a clownish approximation of the New York City skyline, overlooking a miniature version of the Eiffel Tower, on a street that has an escalator instead of a crosswalk.

The heat and the crowds aren't my favorite thing, but I like the way I never have to leave the casino hotels to get everything I need, how I can disappear into them like a pocket universe. It's a city that has the same effect as my work clothes, refracting the spotlight, allowing me to be someone who is just observing the action, not actively participating in it.

The Michelob Ultra Arena, where the Aces play, is connected to Mandalay Bay, where I have a room, and I only have about thirty seconds to strip off my sweats that smell like jet fuel and change into my usual game-day outfit before meeting the Aces' PR team for a facilities tour. In the elevator down, I'm still confirming I have all my essentials—backup charger, backup-backup charger, AirPods, wired headphones—when I get a text from Natalie.

It's a common enough occurrence by now that my heart doesn't stutter. In the two weeks since Natalie first reached out, we've been in regular contact, mostly on days when the Lights aren't playing, when we're both watching other teams. At first, I'd ask a question about a player's performance or Natalie's opinion on someone's coaching style, or she'd complain about a bad call against an old teammate. But our texts have slowly but steadily drifted into non-basketball topics. Opening our message chain, I'm greeted by our exchange from the previous evening.

Natalie: "These girls on TikTok doing full dinner parties . . . I could never. I get exhausted just watching them."

I'd gotten the message while I was eating standing up in my kitchen and responded with a picture of a half-finished chicken parm next to the Trader Joe's box it had come in.

Natalie had responded with a picture of a half-eaten burrito bowl.

Me: "Not Chipotle again."

Natalie: "Why mess with perfection?"

Then her text just now: "Coming through for the press tour? Say hi if so."

Heat bubbles in me, like the jets turning on in a hot tub. All of our messaging thus far has felt safe, with the physical distance between us acting as a buffer against the memory of her hand on my neck, her voice in my ear, and my body's response to both.

I do my best to push the thoughts aside. If I can hide

who I am in forgettable outfits and anonymous hotel bars, I should be able to hide what I want too.

I give a thumbs-up reaction as I exit the elevator and make my way through the casino floor, following the signs to the arena through a hotel that's part corporate convention center and part adult funhouse. When I meet up with the group, there are five other journalists and a publicist. I recognize a duo from *The Athletic* and one from *Defector*, and the last two are joking around with each other and the publicist in a way that implies they're Vegas locals.

When a writer acquaintance—a woman about my age named Sophie who works for a queer website and doesn't usually cover sports—shows up, the publicist starts leading us past the entrance. Sophie falls into step beside me at the back of the pack, and we hug each other in greeting. Though she and I never really hang out, we live in the same small world that's the LA queer scene: We go to the same parties, date each other's exes.

I'm trying to figure out how to tactfully ask Sophie what she's doing here when she heads me off. "I'm working on a piece about the growth of the league from a queer perspective. Off-court stuff like expanded facilities, brand deals, that kind of thing."

"Nice," I say, picturing the UCLA gym. "I just got assigned the Lights as my new beat at the All-Star break."

"That's awesome, congratulations." Sophie raises her brows.

I surprise myself by not wanting to correct her assumption that I would've been begging to cover the WNBA, that this assignment is an upgrade for me, that as a queer woman I'd want to report on a queer women's sport just like she obviously loves covering queer culture. I feel a flicker of guilt, and then some other vaguely empty feeling I don't have a good word for, a sensation like fluorescent lights in an empty warehouse, harsh illumination on what I lack.

"It's been really exciting to learn the game, to just be immersed in the world." It's true, if not the whole truth. I stare straight ahead as we follow the group through the twists and turns of the backstage hallways.

"I love watching all the elder lesbians who are season ticket holders." I can hear the smile in Sophie's voice without looking at her. "They're my favorite people. I just want to hang out with all of them."

I nod, and it's like I can feel the synapses in my brain firing. As a sportswriter, it's important for me to tell stories about the gameplay above all else, but talking to Sophie, I'm realizing how nice it is to tell those stories from within my own community. That observing and writing about the W is, in some way, an immersion into my own cultural history.

"You should pitch that story," I say. "'Catching Up with My Queer Elders at the WNBA Games.' I'd read the shit out of that."

"Oooh, yes." Sophie beams. "I'm absolutely stealing that idea."

The publicist stops us at a set of double doors, waiting for Sophie and me to catch up before launching into a little speech, reminding us that journalists usually aren't allowed in the locker rooms, but they're making an exception so we can report on the expanded facilities as they're actually being used.

"The Aces have extended an invitation to the Lights today too, so those of you who are here from LA can talk to your players if they agree." With that, the publicist shows us into the locker rooms. Unblemished and modern, they look like they'd be stocked with D.S. & Durga hand soap. Sophie and I stick together as we tour exercise rooms and a small cafeteria. In every space, there are large TV screens showing a live stream of the main arena, which is currently in setup mode.

We end with the treatment rooms, where the teams' trainers help players rehab after injuries. We pass a few closed-door sessions and enter a larger open area that smells like lemon and lavender. "The recovery spa," the publicist explains excitedly, pointing out recently installed hot tubs and cold plunges. There are five or six players mostly ignoring us as they soak in full-coverage bathing suits. There isn't anything sexy about the situation at all, really, until I spot Natalie, wearing a sports bra and a small pair of biker shorts, lowering herself into an ice bath and huffing her way through the physical intensity of it. Her stomach muscles quiver as they hit the cold water.

I wonder if it's weirder to look away, like I've been caught seeing something I shouldn't, or to say hello, and before I decide, Natalie spots me. A full grin spreads over her face and she waves. "I'd come say hi," she calls out, "but I have to punish my body for at least another ten minutes."

I smile and shout back, "Gotta keep your edge!"

"Oh my god," Sophie whispers in my ear, "the players—they're all so fucking hot."

It's impossible to answer Sophie. What am I supposed to do, brag that Natalie and I text all the time? Sanctimoniously rebuke the idea of voicing the thought I've obviously had myself? Even just saying "Yeah" makes me feel creepy and guilty, and like I'm lying about something.

Ultimately, it doesn't matter. Sophie is entirely oblivious to my anxiety, and she breaks off to chat with the Aces' team doctor before I need to say anything at all.

As the rest of the group disperses, I linger near the baths, drafting copy in my Notes app while I wait to get a quote from Natalie. It's actually my job to do this, I have to remind myself. Even if it feels like I'm making an excuse to watch her cycle between the hot tub and the cold plunge under the watchful eye of the Lights' staff. After a dutiful ten minutes of contrast therapy, Natalie accepts a towel from her trainer and wraps it around her waist before bounding over to me. The ends of her braids are soaked, dampening her shoulders. She absentmindedly wipes drops of water off the top of her breasts.

For a tense moment I worry that there will be some awkward distance between our digital chatter and our in-person conversation, but Natalie immediately picks up on where our texting left off, telling me that after she'd finished eating her latest Chipotle bowl, she'd started watching *The Traitors* and is already halfway through the latest season.

"Fuck, it'd be so fun to be on the show. I'd be so terrible

at it. But I'd go just to hang out in the castle." She walks us toward the cafeteria, and I grip my phone like it gives me reporterly credibility. Like it explains why we're bantering about reality TV. "I know it can't be technically off the record, but *please* don't print that. I don't want to come off like Scheana Shay, begging to be on *Dancing with the Stars*."

"No promises." I make a stern face. "The readers of the venerable *Los Angeles Chronicle* deserve to know how bad you would be on *Traitors*."

Natalie hip checks me playfully. One of her braids grazes the sleeve of my shirt, leaving a wet streak, a mark where she touched me. "You print one word of that and I'll never call on you during the postgame presser again."

"Pretty sure you're not in charge of that." I narrow my eyes at her and follow her into the cafeteria.

"'I'm just here so I won't get fined,'" Natalie says in a shockingly accurate impression of Marshawn Lynch.

I want to joke back, but instead I force myself to switch into work mode. "Speaking of quotes, though, I do want to get something about the facilities for today's pieces." When I remind myself what I'm supposed to be doing here, using a source to get a quote, it's easier to put the kind of distance between myself and Natalie that I know I need to maintain.

She nods, asks a few quick questions about the story I'm working on, and gives me what I need while choosing her taco bowl toppings.

The Aces' publicist taps me on the shoulder, signaling that it's time for all the journalists to clear out, and Natalie bumps my elbow with hers in goodbye. On my way out, I watch as Natalie heads toward a table, then sees an Aces player pulling up a chair. Natalie gives her a tight smile, then turns away, sitting somewhere else.

My first instinct is to clock this, note a potential storyline—rivals make great pieces. My second instinct is to forget I saw anything, to protect whatever private beef Natalie is harboring. Following the publicist out of the locker room, I have a queasy feeling in my stomach. I've been friendly with players before, but I've never allowed my personal feelings about them to affect what I write.

IX

For the first half of the game, Sophie sits next to me on press row, taking a few notes and shouting happily at the very Vegas-style pyrotechnics that shoot off above the baskets. But mostly, she bounces her leg and cracks her knuckles, twitches I assume are indications that the actual gameplay bores her. Then during halftime, she touches my shoulder and says apologetically, "I'm going to see if I can take an empty seat somewhere else—it's killing me not to be able to cheer." *Cheer for what?* I think. The Lights are getting trounced by the Aces, who are up by more than twenty. But I nod as if I understand, and during the third quarter I see she has found a way to sit even closer to the court and is chanting along with a pair of those elder-dyke season ticket holders, both wearing A'ja Wilson jerseys. When Wilson hits a three-pointer, she jumps to her feet screaming.

I realize Sophie doesn't have team loyalty, doesn't care who wins or loses. She is here for the environment, the culture, the vibes. It's not how I consume sports—frankly, I find casual fandom both baffling and sacrilegious—but at the same time, watching her fills me with a sort of familial warmth, like walking into the home I grew up in. The WNBA carved out a place for queer fans to feel safe and welcome, and it's starting to make me wonder if being queer could be part of my professional identity rather than something incidental and unrelated. I think, *This would never happen in the NFL*, and for the first time, the thought makes me feel happily dazed.

When Natalie makes a clutch three-point shot over the head of the Aces' defender, the shouts of "Natty Ice!!!" echo from the pockets of Lights fans in the crowd. Grateful for the distraction, I turn my focus back to my notes, watching the Lights make great moves on a few beautiful possessions before succumbing to their inevitable loss.

During the press conference, I finish and file my gamer—with a little extra meat from today's tour—and jot down some thoughts for a heftier piece on the discrepancies between teams' facilities and how that might impact player performance.

Back at the hotel, I put in a perfect room service order—a Caesar salad, french fries, and a dirty gin martini—and nestle into the bed, hoping the NFL Network has some good classic games on-demand.

I'm watching the 1982 49ers win their first-ever Super Bowl against the Cincinnati Bengals when my phone lights up with a photo from Natalie.

In focus, her big hand, holding five cards. Fuzzy in the

background, a poker table and a dealer putting down the third card in the flop of what is obviously a game of Texas Hold 'Em.

My mind leaps to something a dyke friend once told me: "When a girl sends you a picture of her fingers, that's basically a dick pic."

"Do you know how to play this game?" Natalie texts.

"Yup," I thumb back as I pull the covers tighter.

Natalie: "I lost $300 in like five minutes somehow."

Natalie: "Please get down here and help."

Oh my god, I think. "Oh my god," I text. I consider my next move and let myself follow my impulse. "Where are you?"

As I get out of bed and throw all the clothes from my suitcase across it, half of my brain starts screaming, *She's hot, wear something sexy!* and the other half is begging, *This is a professional contact and you need to act like it*. I decide to blame the martini when I put on a white tank top that I'd brought to sleep in. It's technically decent, but I know that under the casino lights the barest outlines of my nipples will be visible to anyone who chooses to look hard enough. It's the kind of thing I would wear to a queer party in LA.

I know where the line is, and as I inch closer to it, I trust myself not to cross it—to put my career first. Not only does the *Chronicle* have an ethics policy against romantic entanglements with sources, but all of my peers would immediately turn on me. I wouldn't just be fired, I'd be unhirable.

But actively trying to look good isn't against any rules.

The actual worst-case scenario here is just that giving myself over to my crush on Natalie Czapski is an incredibly quick and thorough way to hurt my own feelings. And I've never not done something just to spare my own feelings.

Identifying how I experience my emotions has always been a challenge for me. I hate it when my therapist asks me where, physically, I am feeling something. I always want to snap back, "I don't know, in my brain???" But I have never had a problem sensing desire in my body. I feel it as a restless buzz in my fingers and toes, as a tugging underneath my ribs that threatens to literally pull me forward, as a liquid warmth that pools in my stomach, and as a second, much more intense heartbeat that thumps ferociously from some place deep in my pelvis. A pulsation that makes me feel like a string instrument being played by a strong hand. If I look at someone and feel that hum, I know I am absolutely fucking gone for them, at least physically. I have it for Natalie, badly enough that I'll go to her when called.

After one last glance in the mirror, I check my texts.

"I'm in the Mandalay Bay casino?" Natalie has sent back.

Me: "I'm going to need you to be more specific. Don't bet on anything until I get there. Unless you're dealt a pair of Aces or Kings."

Natalie: "I'm in the poker room. Go left when you get in. What's your drink order?"

Me: "Gin martini, dirty, two olives."

I pocket my phone as the elevator opens into the lobby. I find my way into the mazelike casino and flag down a cocktail waitress, who gives me excellent directions to the cashier's cage and then the poker room. I tip her for her trouble. I take out $200 in chips—barely enough to play with in Vegas but all I'm willing to part with, and hopefully enough to keep me at the table with Natalie for a little while, if I catch a few lucky hands.

When I veer left through the poker room, the first thing I spot is a sweating martini glass at a vacant seat, then the back of Natalie's head. Her hair is pulled back into her two tight French braids, neat enough that she must have redone them after her postgame shower. She's wearing a thin black tank top, and all the tattoos on her shoulders are visible.

My heartbeat picks up as I slide into the chair in front of the glass and put my chips on the table.

"Jen, you made it." She turns in her chair and wraps her arms around me in a big, friendly hug, which only dips into flirty when she whispers in my ear, "I think I'm in over my head here." She doesn't seem tipsy to me, but I'm a little buzzed myself, which means we're probably right on that same level. I hug her back as passionlessly as I can muster and survey the scene.

At the opposite side of the table, a couple is exchanging sweet little kisses, absorbed in each other's company. A seat down from Natalie, an older guy chats with the dealer about world history. The screen shows that the small blind is $10 and the big blind is $15, probably the lowest on the strip. I relax. Nobody is at this table to *really* gamble.

"You're good at this?" Natalie asks, taking a sip of her drink, a glass of rosé that looks small in her big hand. I can't help but smile at her unpretentious, almost dorky beverage choice. It makes her seem basic—approachable and sweet—which puts me at ease almost as much as the low price of admission at the table.

"I'm not going to win the World Series of Poker any time soon, but I know how to play."

"Thank god. Because I need serious help."

The dealer pauses her conversation on the aerodynamics of World War II bombers and starts dealing, nodding at me for the small blind. I put in a $10 chip as I explain to Natalie how blinds work. She nods along and tosses her chips in.

"Okay, first," I take a sip of my martini, still cold enough to taste fantastic, "is there a maximum amount you'd want to lose, if you lose? An amount where you'll wake up and not feel like shit about it?"

Natalie considers and I brace myself for the answer, contemplating where that number might land. Natalie played in college before students were allowed to make sponsorship deals, so the rookies coming into the W now are already millionaires in a way that wasn't available to her. But she's been a big star in the WNBA for more than five years now, and therefore is basically a rich person, so she is going to give a rich-person answer.

"Like, three thousand dollars maybe? That would be a lot, but I would be okay."

I feel a sting on my own behalf knowing she could lose in one night more than a month of my rent. But then I feel a sting on her behalf knowing that if I'd been sitting next to one of my NFL player sources, the amount would've been ten—or one hundred—times that.

"Good to set your limits verbally before you start," I say, sitting up straighter.

She leans toward me, like she did at the All-Star after-party, even though it's not loud here. "I'm a big fan of communication," she says, her voice low, and I laugh and turn back to the cards in front of me.

For the next hour, we play lazy, silly poker. Neither the dealer nor the other players seem to care that I'm not being dealt in every time and am instead helping Natalie recognize when she might have a chance at two pairs or a straight, and when she needs to fold. She leans into my space to show me her cards, and so that I can whisper instructions in her ear. We get giggly drunk on our martinis and rosé, and she sings low in her growly voice, *"You gotta know when to hold 'em, know when to fold 'em,"* which strikes me as hilarious. It's the kind of flirting I hope for on a good first date, when we're getting along well enough that I know, by the end of the night, the woman I'm out with is going to let me touch her. I have to remind myself that I'm not going to get to touch Natalie.

When Natalie gets the hang of the game enough that we can each play on our own, I lean out of her space to look at my own cards. But her hand chases our previous closeness, settling somewhere near my knee. As I curl up the edges of my cards to see what I've been dealt, Natalie runs her finger along the inseam of my black jeans. The touch is low enough on my leg that it isn't necessarily indecent, but it's undeniably intimate. Desire pulses low in my belly. We barely shift for the next few hands, quietly playing cards while Natalie's finger rubs lightly but insistently against my lower inner thigh. I feel myself getting wet against the cotton of my underwear. I know I should move, but the mood is so heady and the ache so sweet I can't bring myself to stop it.

When Natalie finally lifts her fingers to reach for her glass, I feel like I've been simultaneously freed and deprived. Then her arm snakes around my shoulders and her fingertips land at the place where my shoulder and neck meet.

She leans closer. "How did you learn to play poker?"

"A lot of the sportswriters at the *Chronicle* play." I'm surprised at how steady my voice sounds; I was expecting it to stutter in sync with my pulsating heart. "Before smartphones, playing cards was a good way to pass the time on road trips. And everyone's competitive."

When it's my turn to bet, I raise, hoping a few people at the table will come along with me. I have three of a kind, and I could win enough to keep playing for a while longer. Natalie folds, and her always-moving fingers start rubbing the seam of my tank top, making gestures big enough that she touches the warm skin on my neck. She likes the texture of the stitching, maybe. Or how warm my skin is. My underwear is getting slicker.

"So you play to blend in? Or because you actually like it?" It's a more astute question than I expect from her at this moment, with the buzz of alcohol and touch.

"A little bit of both," I say, and repaying her intimacy with honesty makes my head go light.

The rest of the players call and I win the hand. I barely notice. My eyes are locked on the green felt, but all of my attention is focused on the light brushes of her fingers against my pulse point just under my jawline.

"You do a lot of stuff to blend in, don't you?" Her nails graze the fuzzy little hairs of my undercut. "You keep this hidden."

My breath stutters in response to her touch. "It's not like I'm in the closet. I just don't want anyone I'm covering to think anything about me for more than a second."

Natalie cocks her head, looking at me harder than she had before. I've surprised her.

"It's kind of like me and basketball." She nods. "Most of the time, I don't want to think about anything except the game."

"Is that why you don't date?" I'm helpless against the question, and I wince at my transparency.

She smirks, visibly amused. "'Basketball is my wife,'" she says, mocking herself. "I sounded like an asshole."

I shrug. "Nah, that kind of line sells papers. Metaphorically speaking."

Natalie's fingers still, then tap once on my shoulder, deliberate enough that we can't pretend her touches are absentminded anymore. I turn away from the game.

"I want to tell you why I don't date, but—and I'm sorry I have to say this—the conversation would have to be off the record."

The intimacy we've been building shatters a little, like a rock hitting a window and the glass cracking in concentric circles.

"I won't be writing about tonight." Saying it makes

me feel embarrassed and a little stupid, to have forgotten myself when Natalie certainly hasn't. Now I wonder if her cute rosé was her just avoiding drinking anything harder, trying to stay relatively sober around me. I try to move away from her arm, to give ourselves the appropriate distance, but she holds on to my shoulder, lightly, not locking me in place but asking me to stay.

Natalie exhales. Bites her lip. "I have to be careful."

And even though it makes me feel like shit, I know she's right. Her personal life might not make *Us Weekly*, but it would definitely get talked about on podcasts and TikTok and, if the gossip was salacious enough, maybe even Deuxmoi.

I nod, businesslike. I decide I've had enough gin to shake off the feeling of embarrassment and rejection. "Noted, off the record. Go on."

"Ladies," the dealer interjects, softly exasperated. We'd stopped paying attention and have finally pushed the limits of what the table will allow.

We shove some chips into the middle of the board and start going through the motions again. Natalie's hand drops from my shoulder back down to my leg, higher this time, her index and pointer finger moving in lazy circles against the meat of my inner thigh. Her touch feels like half apology, half yearning.

"In college, I told myself I was too busy. Practice, games, and classes too—I wasn't into that 'D's get degrees' bullshit. I wanted to make the most of all the things I was being given. It didn't leave room to think about dating."

"So what? You were celibate?" I'm proud of myself for the skepticism and self-possession in my voice, despite the pulses of desire zinging through my body.

She laughs low and a little cocky, her hand creeping even higher. "Just because I didn't date doesn't mean I didn't have any fun. But a real relationship? No. I don't know why it doesn't work for me when it's fine for everyone else, but when I'm dating, I don't play as well. I tried to get serious with a few girls, and every time, I'd get on a cold streak with my shooting, or my grades would slip. I wanted to take school and basketball seriously, so I stopped trying to make something happen romantically."

She folds. "And then I got drafted into the W, and there was so much work to do. It was easy not to date—easy to just, you know, talk to girls. Then a few years ago, I looked around me and saw that people on my team didn't just have girlfriends; they had wives. Or husbands. And they were having kids. I thought, *Why not me?*"

Natalie pauses as a waitress walks by, gesturing toward our empty glasses. I ask the bartender to switch me to beer. Natalie rubs the palm of her hand fondly across the length of my thigh, scratching at the denim a little with her nails, before resuming those light, teasing inner thigh touches. I feel like I'm going to catch on fire.

"So I started dating Allison. In college, we were close friends, and a few months after I started thinking about whether I might be ready for a relationship, she and her girlfriend broke up, and so, I don't know. I asked her out to dinner and she said yes."

"Wait"—a few dots connect in my gin-fuzzed brain—"Allison Altman, like, the player who just retired from the Aces?" The pretty player Ashley had steered me away from at the All-Star party.

Natalie nods, then she takes her hand away from me, and I feel the loss like a gut punch, until I see she's just getting our drinks from the waitress, whom she tips with a $20 chip.

"For a while it was really good." She smiles small at the memory. "It made me feel like a real person, not just like, 'eat, sleep, play basketball,' you know? I was really gone for her.

"I thought about her a lot. I thought about her all the time. When I was at home, when I was training." Natalie pauses, sucks in a breath. "I thought about her while I was playing too. Especially when we were playing the Aces. So, of course, I was thinking about her a lot that night.

"Alli said something to me on the court, something flirty, just like, 'Can't wait until this game is over and I get to take you home.' That tipped me over the edge. I wasn't just thinking about her; she was suddenly *all* I could think about. I was playing distracted; I was thinking about her instead of the game. And that's when I lost my footing."

I flash to the footage I saw of the huddle of Natalie's teammates after her fall, the way a player from Vegas had stayed close to her even though it was unusual for one of the players from the opposing team to do so. I realize that was Allison. I remember watching the moment Natalie realized how serious her injury was, and the way she'd cried when she knew her season was over.

This is what Natalie has been holding back. For her, the

injury wasn't an unpreventable accident, some ill fortune. She thinks it's something she could've prevented, something she should be ashamed of—evidence that she never should've fallen for someone in the first place.

She touches me again, this time running her fingers across the back of my hand, where it's resting on the poker table. I resist the urge to turn my hand over and lace her fingers with my own, or to touch her anywhere that she's been touching me.

"You didn't tear your ACL because you had a girlfriend." My voice is quiet but firm, and my eyes flick from her face to where she's touching me.

"No, you're wrong." Natalie shakes her head vehemently, pulling her hand away. "Sorry, I don't mean to be an asshole, but you're not a player. To play well, you have to be able to put things aside and keep your head clear. I can't do that, and so I got injured. It's not complicated."

I shrug helplessly. It's sort of heartbreaking to see how much shame Natalie is carrying about this. I can also tell there's nothing I can do to convince her otherwise.

"I don't know how long my professional career is going to be, but I know I'll still be young when I can't play basketball anymore. And then I'll be able to date."

I haven't had enough to drink to do anything unethical, but I am off-kilter enough to let thoughts that I'd rather not think flood my head: I want to take whatever spark of attraction exists between us and use it to prove Natalie wrong. I want to wrap my arms around her neck, press the whole of my body against hers and show her that she can have a girlfriend and play excellent basketball. I want to kiss her and date her and watch her absolutely cook on the court until she can't deny that she *can* have both. Something—maybe the gin—gives me the confidence to believe that if she let me, I could turn myself into the exact thing she needs.

It's dangerous to want her, but I can't help it.

"Buying in?" the dealer asks loudly, popping our little bubble and saving me from myself. I push down everything I just let myself think and blink my way back to reality.

The dealer glares pointedly in my direction, and I realize that my paltry stack has dwindled to a single $5 chip, not enough to cover the small blind.

"That was my max to lose today." Before I finish the sentence, Natalie moves her hand away from mine, picks up a $100 chip, and drops it in front of me.

"No," I say automatically. "The *Chronicle* doesn't allow journalists to accept gifts from subjects."

I push the chip back toward her, proud of myself for doing so even though it means giving up my seat at this poker table.

"What about all the food and drinks and stuff from All-Star weekend?"

"Eating hors d'oeuvres paid for by Nike isn't the same, Natalie," I sigh, and there's comfort in expressing frustration with her. "Sticking to my ethics as a journalist is as important to me as you making sure our conversation was off the record."

She nods. Concedes.

"If you're not playing . . ." the dealer says, trailing off.

I get up, and for some reason, I'm a little surprised that Natalie stands up as well. I don't know why I expected her to stay without me, but she shoves her remaining chips in her pocket and grabs her drink. She moves with me a few steps away from the table, and we linger awkwardly, not sure where to go exactly. Natalie catches my arm gently, rubbing the inside of my wrist with her thumb.

"Is that the only rule for writers and their subjects?" She asks the question quietly, looking at my arm instead of in my eyes.

"No," I say, simply and softly. Not aggressive, but insistent.

She drops my wrist. I want to be proud of myself again, but instead I feel bruised and aching.

We walk together, not talking or touching, through the loud and bright casino floor, to the hotel elevator bank. I press the button on the wall, and when the car arrives, Nat holds the doors open with one arm and gestures for me to enter ahead of her. We ride up together, the silence between us thick, standing close enough that the ghost of her touching me is as potent as the caresses themselves were.

X

I've got my big headphones on, and I'm ignoring Sean's frenetic keyboard clicking at the desk next to mine. I just filed a quick news story about Olivia Agwuegbo—the player who had that sensational game—being traded to the Lights to round out our starting lineup, and I'm putting the finishing touches on a draft of my practice facility feature. It's the first WNBA article I've written with a negative bent, contrasting the Lights' shitty setup and lackluster future plans with other teams' modern practice spaces and locker rooms. The implication is that the owners' unwillingness to invest more means the Lights can't attract the talent to make the team a real championship contender. I got a former Lights player to go on the record suggesting that this outdated approach—especially in a post–Caitlin Clark WNBA—is rooted in misogyny. I'm dangerously close to getting a few current Lights to talk on background, speaking to me as anonymous sources. I barely hear the music coming through my ears; I'm radiating the kind of energy that makes my fingers tingle and my words come tumbling out of me, which means I'm writing something good.

As I rearrange two paragraphs to sharpen the argument, I realize that I haven't felt this kind of righteous indignation when constructing a story since last football season, when the Cougars front office traded away their incredible tight end for the dubious talents of an aging quarterback. I'd put in the legwork on the facilities reporting not just because it was a good story, I'm realizing, but also because I care as much about writing about the Lights as I do about the Cougars.

Fifteen minutes after I turn in my draft, David sends me a Slack message. "Got five?"

I take off my headphones and pop into David's office, assuming he wants to go through my latest draft and talk about how we're going to approach the Lights' PR team for comment. David has his sleeves rolled up, which makes him look like Mark Ruffalo playing a newspaper editor in a movie that wishes it was *All the President's Men*.

"You're off the Lights beat," David says without preamble.

For a heart-stopping second, I wonder if David found out Natalie and I were flirting in Vegas and if I'm about to get fired over it.

"You get to go back to the Cougars."

I exhale deeply, but my heart is still stuttering. Maybe it's because I spent the last four hours creating historical timelines for the practice facilities for every WNBA team since the inception of the league in 1997, but I can't quite access the notion that I am getting what I want. Instead, I feel like something is being ripped away from me. This is what I asked for, but it feels like a loss.

"Is the paper going to stop covering the Lights?" I press my palms against my thighs and squeeze.

"I finally convinced the powers that be that we need a basketball writer covering the W. You were always right about that." David's tone is cavalier, conspiratorial, like we've accomplished something together—and we have, actually. How am I supposed to tell him that now I'm not sure I want my prize?

"Your work has been pivotal in helping me convince the higher-ups that we needed to cover the Lights seriously, so we're reassigning Sean. I'm going to tell him as soon as we're finished here.

"You did fantastic work, and without you the paper wouldn't be committing more resources to the league. I'm not going to forget that when it comes to raises and promotions, okay? This is a testament to your success. You get to go back to doing what you want."

"Right." I lick my lips and look at the strip of the 405 through his window before turning back to him and flashing him a big smile that I've learned doesn't read as fake as it feels. "I'd like to finish up the facilities story first." I'm already slipping into the bargaining stage of grief.

David waves a hand in front of my space, as if my words are smoke he's diverting away from his eyes. "Your draft is nearly there; you'll still get the byline." Because he assumes getting a byline for my work is all I care about when it comes to this article. "You don't mind sharing with Sean." A statement, not a question.

"Thank you, David," I force myself to say. "I'm glad

to hear that my work has stood out, and that I get to go back to my NFL assignment." To my ears, I sound like I'm reading from a script.

"Great." His eyes shift back to his computer monitor. "I'm sure you have a lot of catching up to do."

I take that as the dismissal it is meant to be and head back to my desk, trying to act normal.

A Slack notification from Sean: "David just asked me to meet him in his office. Are they doing layoffs?"

I swivel in my chair toward Sean and tap him on the shoulder. He takes out his earbuds.

"I've been put back on the Cougars, and you're going to cover the Lights. Try to act surprised."

"Let's fucking GO," Sean says automatically, punching the air in victory.

"Very subtle." I roll my eyes, but then my deep affection for Sean bubbles up, and it overtakes my unanticipated disappointment. Sean, who stayed up late during All-Star weekend to make sure I was adequately prepared to write my profile of Natalie, and who never once acted pissy about me getting the assignment he should've gotten in the first place. Sean deserves this beat, and he'll be amazing at it. The W and the Lights and Natalie all deserve to have Sean too—and the Cougars deserve me and my years of dedication to them.

"Congrats, babe," I say.

Sean must catch something I can't even detect in my face or in my tone, because his smile drops. "This is what you want, right?"

"Absolutely." I grab his arm and squeeze it encouragingly. "I'm just not emotionally equipped for sudden change. Now go see David and pretend you're astounded to hear this news."

"Sure thing." He rests one hand meaningfully on my shoulder before heading into David's office.

I know he knows there's more to it, and I also know he'll let it go. I turn back to my computer and Slack my group chat with Sean and Casey: "Bar after work??"

Three blocks from the office, there are two bars: an Instagram-fancy cocktail lounge, described by the *LA Chronicle*'s own food section as a "glamorous art deco hideaway," and a dingy-looking windowless den with an ancient neon sign that says "Bar"—and if Bar has any other name, we don't know it. They have enough streaming subscriptions that Sean, Casey, and I can generally watch any sports game we want. The only rule that we have for Bar is that we are never, ever allowed to invite any restaurant writers to come drink with us there, because the place will be overrun and ruined the minute their story hits the internet.

I leave work first and I'm halfway through a dirty gin martini and a basket of fries—morosely watching the young, fast Indiana Fever run over a new expansion team that doesn't have their feet under them yet—before Casey and Sean join me.

"Shots, Brody!" Sean shouts to the bartender, who

always gives us a friends and family discount. Casey says she has a crush on him but refuses to act on it, so as not to ruin the sanctity of Bar.

"We're celebrating!" she chimes in.

"Three shots." Brody reaches for a bottle of tequila without us having to clarify. "What are we celebrating?"

"Four shots," I say, and Brody knows I mean one for him too, which is part of why he loves us. "Sean got a promotion today!"

"And Felix gets to go back to covering the Cougars," Casey adds, sliding into the seat on my left, while Sean takes the seat to my right.

"That too." I prop my elbows on the weathered wood of the bar. "Everything is right again in the world."

The four of us clink our shot glasses together, down the liquor, then bite our limes. My eyes drift to the screen, just in time to watch Caitlin Clark chuck the ball from half court to Kelsey Mitchell, who's sprinting into the paint. Mitchell snatches the ball out of the air and would've deposited it into the bucket easy peasy, if another player hadn't grabbed her. But there's no whistle.

"Oh, come on! That's a fucking foul!" I shout.

"Look at you!" Casey sounds impressed.

"The W is so sick." Sean beams. "I'm so excited."

As I return to my martini, I give Sean my Lights download, as if passing the relay baton to a teammate—not out of the race but just done with my part of the run. I remember the feeling of getting my NFL assignment originally, a coup for a writer so young, a validation that all the effort I had put in amounted to something special. David telling me I was exactly the kind of person he hoped would be inspired by his book. My father calling me to tell me he'd changed his newspaper subscription to the *LA Chronicle* even though he's a Giants fan. Live in the good side.

On the TV, the game clock is paused, and a few of the players are yelling, their teammates holding them back. They should be pissed; it was a foul. I glance away from the screen to my phone, and I see I have a minute-old text from Natalie that says, "this is bullshit."

My first instinct is to ask her what happened, get her insights and perspective. But a pang of loss tugs at me. Responding to her will really be the end of it, the nail in the coffin of my WNBA assignment, and I don't want to deal with that right now. I flip my phone face-down and ask Casey and Sean if they want to stay for trivia.

I leave Natalie on read until the next day, until a few hours before she expects me to show up at Crypto for the Lights game.

Dawdling any longer would put me in asshole territory, and I just spit it out: "I was taken off the Lights beat."

Natalie sends me back a string of interrobangs, and as I'm composing a response, my phone lights up with a FaceTime call from her.

I take a second before answering, close my eyes for a moment to tamp down any fluttery excitement that might be obvious on my face, and then tilt the phone so my front-facing camera will capture the most flattering angle.

Natalie doesn't seem to have put much thought into her phone's vantage point, but even a weird up-the-nose shot doesn't do much to diminish her hotness. Her blond hair is tight in her game-day braids, and she's in the passenger seat of a car, driven by Louisa.

"What the fuck." Her brows are furrowed.

"It's not like that," I say, and I realize I haven't thought through how to present this to her.

She shifts the camera, and she's looking at me now, right in the eyes. She raises a brow as if to say, "Oh really?"

"The coverage of the W has been going so well, our editor was able to justify pulling someone off the NBA. Your new reporter is named Sean, and he's a fantastic basketball writer and a good friend of mine."

"Sean Price? Another white guy, I presume," Louisa says in the background. Natalie's eyes flick to her and then back to me.

"He's been covering basketball for more than a few months," I say, masking my own mixed feelings behind my confidence in Sean. "And not to be like, hashtag not all men, but he's one of the good ones. He's been watching the W for years. He helped prep me for my All-Star weekend assignment. It's a step up for you guys."

"What about you?" Natalie asks.

"I'm going back to covering the Cougars."

"Hmm," she hums. Her phone shifts so it's capturing her profile, and I can't see her eyes. "So that's it then? You're just done?"

I've had to adjust the expectations of sources before, when a story gets killed or changed, so I know what I could say to lighten the vibe and boost her ego. But I don't want to let go of the intimacy and honesty that we cracked open in Vegas. I don't want to pretend with her.

"Honestly? Part of me is happy to be back on the assignment that I spent my entire career working toward. And part of me feels like I'm losing something. Even though I don't get to write about you guys and gay sports anymore, I'm not mad that I just get to be a fan."

I still can't see Natalie's eyes, but I can guess what I'd find in them. I'm familiar now with her serious expression, the way she takes a moment to process something before coming to her conclusion. I wait her out, relieved that my job has made me accustomed to sitting in uncomfortable silences with sources. Still, my core tightens with the threat that this could be it—the end of the road for us.

For a few beats, the only thing I hear is the muffled sound of GloRilla turned way down low.

"Okay. That sounds good then." She moves her hand, and I can see her face again. "You're going to watch tonight?"

"I wouldn't miss it," I say.

"Okay. Great. I gotta go." She hangs up somewhat abruptly, and I contemplate being anxious or upset. But it's game day, and she has to get in her zone.

Fifteen minutes later, another text: an image of a ticket to the Lights game tonight, in the friends and family section. My fingers tighten around the sides of my phone like the device itself is responsible for this gesture.

I draw in a sharp breath as another message from her comes in: "This isn't press row, so I better fucking hear you cheering for me."

XI

I enter Crypto through a VIP entrance I've never had access to before. When I check in with a coordinator, I'm weirdly grateful that she doesn't recognize me as someone who was recently writing about the Lights. My anonymity is a relief. *The players are always giving tickets to friends*, I remind myself. Even if I was dating a player, my attendance here would probably be so unremarkable in this league that it wouldn't even rise to the level of workplace gossip. And like Natalie said herself, just because she doesn't date doesn't mean she doesn't have fun. Who knows how many girls she's invited to games over the years?

Expertly weaving through the arena crowds, the coordinator hands me a wristband before pointing out a group of seats behind the home team's bench and depositing me in a lounge to get snacks and drinks before tip-off.

The space is charmless—outdated leather seats, cocktail tables choked in heavy drapes of velvet fabric the same blue as the Lights' home uniforms, and the persistent smell of buttered popcorn. It's also mostly empty, except for two people at the other end of the bar, one of them wearing what looks like a denim corset with the number 18 painted on the back and the other in a sleek suit. I feel underdressed in black jeans and a plain blue shirt that I threw on thinking it would help me blend in with the fans. The femme in the corset waves to me as the bartender slides an old-fashioned across the bar and I slip him a tip. I lift my plastic cup toward her in greeting and then make my way back to the seats.

Somehow, it hadn't occurred to me that sitting in the friends and family section would have people acting like friends and family, and I approach the two rows of folding chairs—which are arranged so close to the bench that any of us could reach out and touch the players—like I'm solving a complicated logic problem. *Do people have regular spots? Would Natalie want me to sit near her or somewhere out of the way?* I take a seat in the back corner, not ready to fully ingratiate myself with the growing crowd of parents and grandparents, little brothers, boyfriends, and wives.

I feel naked without my full journalistic arsenal, and I'm grateful when my phone buzzes, giving me something to do. A text from Sean: a picture of me from the back, taken a second earlier, and a series of exclamation points.

I quickly type out, "I was just going to text you!"

"Are you in friends and family?"

"Yeah! A goodbye/thank-you thing from the team." I wince at the lie, hating both that I'm being dishonest with him and that it's not even very convincing; it would be very unusual for a team to do something like that, and he would know. "Sorry I didn't tell you. It came up last minute."

"Enjoy life in the cheering section," Sean writes back, just as the arena dims and the announcer bellows, *"Are you ready for your Hollywood Lights!!??"*

The DJ plays a new Doechii single as the Lights' dance crew forms a pulsating tunnel of people around the starting lineup. First comes our new starter, Olivia Agwuegbo, who hopefully will play as well for the Lights as she did for the Sun. Then Jada Jackson, who is playing well enough to contend for Rookie of the Year.

"Standing six foot three, number nine, it's CZ, Natalie Czapski!" A man with a huge camera balanced on his shoulder follows Natalie as she jogs onto the court and into the team huddle, and on the Jumbotron, the camera's feed shows the players sling their arms over each other's shoulders and sway back and forth to the beat. The crowd screams and screams. In the friends and family section, everybody except me is already out of their chair. We never stand up on press row, but now I jump to my feet before anyone notices I wasn't standing already.

The music dies down, and in the quiet moment before tip-off, as the team gathers around their coach, Natalie's head pops up over the huddle and she scans the seats until she finds me. She locks her eyes with mine and gives me that big smile. Because I want to, because I can, I smile back.

During the first quarter, I quietly watch the Lights trade

the lead with the Chicago Sky half a dozen times, unable to shake off the idea that I can't be seen cheering. Toward the end of the second, Natalie sinks a difficult turnaround jump shot to regain the lead, and when everyone around me launches up, whooping, erupting into cheers, I see Natalie glance at me, still seated and quiet, as she runs past her bench. A few seconds later, the coach pulls her for a quick rest, and after squeezing half a bottle of blue Gatorade into her mouth and scrubbing a towel over her face, Natalie twists around in her chair and flashes that mischievous, cocky grin at me.

"You know it's weirder if you don't cheer, right?" She shouts.

"I'll take that under advisement," I shout back, trying to match her bluster but feeling heat rise in my cheeks.

The Sky close out the quarter with a brutal ten-point run, and I can see the frustration on Natalie's face. Ten seconds before the half ends, Natalie cuts deep into the paint and Jada splits two defenders, bouncing a pass to Natalie, who makes the easy layup. It's beautiful basketball, but it doesn't feel like enough. When the buzzer sounds, Natalie jogs into the tunnel without glancing back.

During halftime, I find my way back to the courtside lounge, where I load up two paper carriers with hot dogs and candy. I meet Sean in the lobby, where he gratefully accepts the food away from the nosy, prying eyes of our fellow reporters.

We exchange some analysis of one of the Lights' bench players and talk a little about how Olivia's game is evolving.

The conversation stays safely in the realm of game talk, until—

"Pretty weird for the team to give you a friends and family ticket, right?" he says between mouthfuls of hot dog.

He's giving me an opening, and I'm not ready to take it. "I've gotta pee before the second half begins," I say, squeezing his elbow and fleeing without answering.

For the first five minutes of the third quarter, I watch the action intently, clapping along to celebrate the Lights' buckets and strong defensive maneuvers. Even down by eight, the Lights are cleaner than they used to be—switching tighter off the pick-and-roll, contesting shots without fouling, keeping the Sky's ball handlers a step outside the paint. A few weeks ago, I wouldn't have even caught the difference. I would've just thought they were playing "harder." Now I can see the plan, the way they are trying to claw their way back into it, playing possession by possession. It makes my chest buzz the same way it does when I watch the Cougars execute a perfect blitz scheme.

Then, as the shot clock hits zero, Natalie sinks a three-pointer, and I'm on my feet without thinking about it. I scream and thrust three fingers in the air in time with the crowd around me, and it feels so good. Like I'm part of this: participating, not just observing. Showing my cards. Natalie looks for me as she jogs backward for the next possession, her gaze like a live wire snapping across the court. During her next rest, she twists around in her seat. "That's more fucking like it."

The Lights step up their defense, end the third tied, and

go on an offensive run to start the fourth quarter. It's enough for a decisive ten-point win, and I feel absurdly proud that the team did so well during Sean's first game covering them. As if I have anything to do with their success.

As the crowd filters out of the arena, I get two text messages nearly simultaneously.

From Sean: "Meet for a drink after I file?"

From Natalie: "Stick around for a little, while I finish up here?"

To Sean, I respond: "Next time?"

To Natalie: "See you soon."

XII

Amid the regular guests in the courtside lounge having a round of champagne, I hang back, drinking a beer, content to be semi-ignored and left on the edges of the revelry. Wins are a bit rarer than any Lights fan would like, and those who are intimately connected with the team aren't about to miss an opportunity to celebrate. I alternate between people watching and searching social media for clips of Natalie's three-pointer as the toasting peaks and the crowd dwindles.

When Natalie shows up, there are just a couple of stragglers remaining—a player's parent, a bartender—and they leave before we have to decide how to behave in front of onlookers.

When the door clicks shut behind them, Natalie flashes me a smile that's simultaneously cocky and shy. I realize that we haven't been alone together since Vegas. I then realize, more deeply, that we've actually never been *truly* alone until now. I intend to thank her for the tickets and ask her how the presser went, wondering if she had spoken to Sean at all. I have my talking points prepared, and I mentally cling to them like a security blanket. But the air hangs heavy between us, and it's clear we aren't going to make small talk.

"Can I ask you a question?" She takes a step toward me. We're still standing weirdly far away from each other, opposite sides of an empty room.

Before I can say something neutral like *Sure*, the word "Anything" escapes my mouth.

"If you've been reassigned back to the Cougars, is there still a rule about this?" She wags her pointer finger back and forth between us.

I suck my bottom lip between my teeth. "It's a gray area." There isn't a rule against it anymore, but if I do this—whatever this is—I probably won't be able to write about the W again.

I toe the ground in front of me, then look at her. "But no, not really. I'm free to do whatever I want."

Natalie moves across the room so fast I barely have enough time to think the phrase *She's a professional athlete* before her body is up against mine. She rubs a thumb over my lips, but that's the extent of her patience. She bends over me, but I still have to stand on my toes to reach her mouth, and when we finally kiss, the desire that ripples through my body is like the loudest, deepest drumbeat I've ever heard. I'd been pushing my desire out of my mind as much as I could, but my body knows how long I've been waiting.

Natalie slides her hands against my hips and sucks my bottom lip into her mouth, wetting my lips with her tongue, as the pulses of longing settle deep between my legs. Then she moves on to my neck.

"I've wanted to do this for so long," she says against my throat. "Before Vegas."

"Since when?" I'm hungry to know if she wants me as much as I want her. How deep her yearning goes. I wrap my arm around her and suck at her neck, enough for her to feel something but not so hard as to leave a mark that would be obvious on TV tomorrow.

"Since the All-Star game," she says, and I know when she means—when I told her the truth to get her to talk to me.

She slips her hand underneath the hem of my shirt and rubs the swath of skin between my belly button and my hip.

"It was before that for me," I say deliriously, like her touch is forcing me to come clean to both her and myself.

"Since when?" she asks, echoing me, as her hand climbs my torso, rubbing against the smooth fabric of my T-shirt bra, searching for my nipple. My breasts, on the smaller side, have never felt quite as sexy as they do now, each a perfect handful in Natalie's broad palm.

"Since the Skims shoot." I retain enough composure not to confess how my body responded to her the first time I saw her take the court.

She laughs into my hair, as if proud of herself and how good she looked that day. She gives up on finding my nipple under my bra and pushes the fabric aside. Breathing hard, I wrap my hands around my back, under my shirt, unhook it, and try to wrangle it off.

Natalie watches me struggle with a small smile, then slides her hands into the sleeves of my T-shirt to help me. She tugs my bra free, tosses it onto the floor, shoves my shirt up. She kisses my collarbone and then sucks a nipple into her mouth. I can't bite back a strangled panting noise, the sensation zinging like a circuit down to my clit.

She pulls her mouth off my breast and maneuvers us toward the bar where they were serving beers just a few minutes earlier. In one swift motion, she lifts me up and sets me down, my legs spread around her. Our faces are level now, and her lips lock onto mine. One hand grips my hip, and the other snakes under my shirt to my breast again, her fingers circling and pinching my nipple, sending jolts of electricity ricocheting through my body. She starts to move her hand away, but I grab it and hold her there, showing her how much I like it when she touches me like that. She slides her tongue into my mouth, groaning like she loves doing it.

I don't think about anything but Natalie, standing in front of me, right now. I pull her hand off my hip and, breaking the wet kiss, I bring her fingers to my mouth. She tugs at my lower lip, and I lick at the tips of her pointer and middle fingers, as her other hand works at my nipple. I open my mouth and she slips her fingers inside. I suck on them while my hands scramble to unbutton and then unzip my jeans, loosening them as much as possible while I'm perched on this surface.

I pull her fingers out of my mouth with a wet pop and guide them down my stomach, past the elastic waistband of my underwear, to my clit, which is slippery and ready. She goes easily where I direct her, as if grateful to be shown exactly how to touch me. She rubs against my clit a little tentatively. "Harder," I say in her ear as softly as I can manage. She finds the ideal pressure, and I say, "Just like that," then press my teeth against the shoulder seam of her T-shirt so I won't make the kind of noise that's loud enough to draw someone into the room.

"Fuck," she says, low in her throat. "Do you always get so wet?"

"Oh yeah, constantly," I gasp into her neck, teasing. "It's really easy to get me going."

She pinches my nipple sharply and chuckles at my yelp.

I kiss her jawline, lick the spot behind her ear, and whisper, "No one gets me as soaked as you do. As watching you does." I exaggerate my delivery to play it off like it's a line. To hide my bafflement at how close it is to true.

"That's more like it." She kisses me wetly, and her fingers slip lower to tease at my opening. "Do you like it here?" she asks.

In response, I jut my hips forward to try to make it easier for her to access me.

"Relax," she murmurs, her fingers teasing in circles. "I got you." With her other hand and all her strength, she shifts my body and adjusts the tilt of my pelvis until her fingers are buried completely inside me and the firm base of her palm is pressed deliciously against my clit. I'm just full enough and the pressure is so right, it's like her hand was made to fuck me like this. With her other hand at my lower back, she guides me to move against her palm while her knuckles curl inside me.

"Here?" Her lips push against my neck, her teeth nipping at that sensitive skin.

"Just a little to the left," I pant. She adjusts, and I cry out, needlessly responding, "There, there."

I wrap my arms around her neck and press my hips forward in jerky circles again and again and again, giving myself the exact pressure and friction on my clit that I need.

She kisses me on my mouth, sloppy and sharp, the way I'm learning she likes to kiss.

She pauses for a moment, her mouth hot against my ear. "Would you say my name when you come?"

When I don't answer right away, she bites my lobe. "Please?"

"Yes," I gasp. Of course I will. As if I didn't want to say her name as I came when she spent an entire evening in Vegas driving me insane. Or when she touched me for the first time at the after-party. Or from the moment I first laid eyes on her.

"Just your first name?" I try to joke, but my voice sputters over my smirk.

She laughs, heavy and low. "If you can get my last name out, I'm not doing it right."

I throw my head back, and within minutes, I say her name over and over and over as my pussy tightens around her fingers and I gush as I come.

I go boneless, letting myself slump forward, pressing my chest into hers, nudging the collar of her shirt aside so

I can suck gently at the skin of her clavicle. She trails her hand at my back up my spine into the fuzz of my undercut.

She slips her fingers out from inside me, making just enough space between us so she can move her hand up to her mouth. The way her head is tilted, I can hear but not see her suck on the wetness there.

I moan as my nipples go hard. "Can you try to be a little less sexy right now?"

She sucks performatively loudly and pulls her fingers out of her mouth, then braces me by my shoulders, holding us far enough apart so she can kiss me softly on the lips, sweet and chaste compared to the way she just fucked me so thoroughly. "Nope," she says, and I barely remember what she's responding to.

"Come back to mine?" She holds my gaze. She might be holding her breath.

"What? You don't want to keep fucking in the visitor's lounge of your place of business?"

She laughs, and I pull myself together as best I can, scooping my bra up from the floor and stuffing it into my bag, buttoning my jeans, and letting Natalie hold my hand as she leads me out of the arena.

When we pull into the lot at her apartment, I try to focus on taking in the scenery instead of questioning what exactly I'm doing here or what it means that Natalie walked me from the arena to staff parking and then drove me to her home. I'm expecting an ugly downtown high-rise, with the kind of gray laminate flooring people make fun of on TikTok, but her building is close to the Arts District, has Art Deco design touches in the lobby and an elevator with an ancient cage door that has to close all the way before it will move. The old-LA details are probably more evidence that the Lights owners aren't investing as much as they should in the team, but still, I appreciate the charm.

The elevator rattles as we rise slowly to the eleventh floor, and Natalie presses me gently against the wall, its authentically distressed mirror reflecting a few blond fly-aways frizzing at her temples. I tug at the hem of her soft white T-shirt and suck her bottom lip between my teeth until we jerk to a stop at her floor.

In Natalie's living room, I catch a glimpse of a huge television set and an even bigger couch, almost a facsimile of my own setup. Before I can get a closer look, she hustles me toward the back of her apartment.

"C'mon," she says, "dirty dishes in the sink are not sexy."

The walls of her bedroom are bare, but her bed is huge and cozy-looking: four pillows, multiple blankets. She falls onto her back and pulls me on top of her. I slot one leg on either side of her hips, like there had been no pause at all between my orgasm and now, and kiss her until we're both gasping.

"Can I take this off?" I tug at her shirt.

She nods and lifts herself up to help me, then reclines with her arms stretched behind her, giving me space to explore the curves of her little breasts, the tattoos across her sternum and ribs, the soft skin stretched across the hard muscles of her stomach. Having caught glimpses of her chest clad in sports bras and framed by the lapels of her nothing-underneath blazers, seeing her without a shirt is almost overwhelming, like she is telling me a secret. I want more.

"Now these?" I play at the waistband of her loose athletic shorts, then her underwear. "Both?"

She bites her lip, nods, and lifts her hips as I take them off her in one go so she's naked under me.

I slide my hand slowly down her torso, holding eye contact, making sure everything I'm doing is something she wants. I ignore the little pulses of desire that palpitate through my stomach. I want to focus on her. I want to show her how good I am at figuring out what she needs and giving it to her.

Along her side and down the curve of her hip is a bruise that looks like a topographical map of a river, deep purple in the middle, with green and yellow at the edges. It's probably from a rough fall she took in the first quarter. I'd known that players get banged up, but I'd never seen something like this bruise firsthand. My fingers run over it tentatively. She hisses a little, but her eyes glaze over with heat. I file that information away for later.

My hand reaches the warm space between her legs. I move slowly, my touch asking her what she wants before giving it to her. "Just on my clit, okay?" Her voice has an almost dreamy quality.

"Of course," I say, low. "Is it okay if I feel how wet you are?"

Her eyes flutter closed and she nods. I slip my fingers between her folds, and my own lids close at the slickness I find there before bringing my attention back to her clit.

"Tell me how it feels," I kiss her on her neck, her shoulders, her lips. "I want to make it good for you."

She talks me through it—"faster" and "more" and "that, that right there"—until her breath gets ragged. With one arm around her shoulders and the other hand moving in quick, firm circles against her, I suck on that same red spot on her throat I had in my mouth at the arena. Her back arches, and she cries out. Her arms wrap around me, squeezing hard, and her hips jerk. I can't look away from her, from how I made her lose control in my arms. I feel almost smug about how good I was at getting her there, about how good I am at fulfilling her needs.

I keep the pressure up, coaxing her through the longest orgasm I can manage, until she's squirming.

She loosens her grip on me and pushes my fingers off her. "Too much, too much. I can't take any more," she says, laughing.

She sits up, holding on to my thighs so I stay straddled around her, and kisses me, sucking on my bottom lip. Now that Natalie has gotten her fill, I remember my own body. I can feel the blood thudding between my legs, and my hips strain helplessly.

"You want more?" She runs her fingertips down the front of my jeans, teasing.

"Yes, please," I whisper.

She smiles big. "You've got too many clothes on."

She undresses me devastatingly slowly, like she's savoring it. Then, with all that strength and agility and nearly a foot of height on me, she rolls me onto my back. With a knee and her fingers between my legs, she helps me rock into the pressure. When I'm close, she growls in my ear, "The walls are thick in here, you can be as loud as you need to be."

And I don't have to be asked again to give her what she wants, shouting her name when I come.

XIII

The next morning it's Saturday, and by some miracle, we both have the day off. Or at least, the Lights don't have official practice, but I don't know many athletes who truly take a break. After a bit of sleeping in, Natalie kisses me on the forehead and whispers in my ear that she's going to pop down to the gym for a quick run. I plug my phone into her charger, doze a little longer, then snoop as much as I can in Natalie's sparsely decorated apartment.

If I had stayed the night at the home of anyone other than a professional athlete, I'd be mildly alarmed by the lack of personal effects, but for someone who can be traded at the drop of a hat, the less to pack, the better. On the nearly empty bookshelf in the living room, I find a creased stack of Anne Rice's vampire novels and a Tamsyn Muir fantasy series I haven't read myself but have heard described as "really good lesbian necromancer books." It's a reminder that as a rule, the coolest, swaggiest athletes usually harbor at least one dorky hobby.

I open her fridge, and in contrast to the rest of her space, it's stuffed full. At eye level, there's string cheese, bagged salads, a half-picked-apart rotisserie chicken. The bottom shelf is stuffed with paper takeout cartons, and on top of them sits a huge bunch of carrots with the tops still attached, giving the entire fridge a fresh, vegetal smell.

Going through her things—the things that don't strike me as private, at least—is like having a conversation about Natalie with one of her close friends, and with each sniff of her lavender-scented hand soap and glance at her meticulously cared-for sneaker collection, more pieces of Natalie come into focus. And with each little bit of her that I catch a glimpse of, the stronger the push-pull gets of wanting more of her and knowing I can only have this little taste.

I wait until I'm done with my tour to check my phone, anticipating correctly that I'll find texts from Sean and Casey checking in on what I did after the game. Whatever is happening with Natalie is too tenuous to share with even my closest friends, and I respond with something vague: "All that cheering wore me out." What I don't say is that it also turned me on.

When Natalie comes back post-workout in just shorts and a sports bra, perspiration glimmering on her forehead and in the cuts of her arm muscles, I crowd her against the wall and breathe in her scent. I play it like it's a bit, unsure how she'll respond to my genuine desire.

"I like the way your sweat smells," I say, sucking at the skin above her armpit.

"You're a little bit of a pervert, huh?" Her tone is mocking, but she leads me to her couch and lets me lay her down and lick the salt and exertion off her inner thighs.

We fuck, we go to brunch on some sceney downtown rooftop bar, and we go back to her apartment to fuck some more. I tease her about her books, and when she responds with "What do you read, sports memoirs?" I just blush. I let her suck bruises onto parts of my body that will be hidden under my clothes. Time gets liquid. We nap, we ravage her leftovers, and we fuck one more time as the big California sun sinks into the ocean, leaving the sky pink and orange. And as the light fades, the mood shifts.

Natalie climbs out of bed and starts to get dressed in a clean T-shirt and basketball shorts, leaving me naked under her comforter. "Our practice is pretty early tomorrow," she says with her back to me.

She's not being subtle, and I'm not an idiot. For some reason, after pursuing me and sleeping with me and extending our date into more than twenty-four hours, Natalie Czapski is giving me the brush-off.

I'm not immune to the sting of rejection, and self-protective, defensive, reactionary thoughts are the first to bubble up: Lesbians can be fuckboys too, especially famous ones. I read too much into this, and I should know better. She isn't attracted to me; she's attracted to the chase, and now that she's sexually sated, she's done.

But Natalie hasn't been acting like the fuckboy dykes I've dated in the past, who have said to my face without any shame that they were just really busy this weekend and maybe they'd hit me up the weekend after, or the weekend after that. No, Natalie is averting her eyes; her shoulders are high and tense with anxiety. She slips out of the bedroom, like she's incapable of staying near me. This isn't fuckboy behavior, it's something else.

Natalie and I have texted enough that she knows a lot of things about me. But maybe she hasn't known me long enough—doesn't yet know me well enough—to understand that one of my primary personality traits, and something I'm secretly very proud of, is my adaptability. I'm very, very good at figuring out what people need, and besides writing, nothing in my life feels quite as good as figuring out what someone is seeking and giving it to them.

I stumble out of bed as quickly as I can, throwing on my underwear and T-shirt for dignity's sake, and follow Natalie into the kitchen, where she's chugging from a huge glass jar full of water. I lean against the counter, looking at her even though she won't look at me.

I want to tell her she's being a childish idiot, but I swallow that temptation—thank god for therapy. "I'll fuck off if you want me to, but I'm going to need you to tell me that's what you actually want." I jut my chin forward and let myself sound bold.

Natalie flicks her eyes over to me, one brow shooting up, but then shifts her attention back to the sink, the dirty dishes. Instead of answering me, she turns on the hot water, opens the dishwasher, and drops the door between us.

"I know you're not interested in dating." I stay planted, on the verge of being in her way. "I haven't forgotten our conversation in Vegas."

Natalie tenses as if she can't help it, then relaxes like it's a reflex she's honed. "It's not about whether or not I'm *interested* in dating." She emphasizes the word *interested* like she's going to expand on that, but instead she aggressively scrubs our plates.

"My point is, I'm not going to ask you for anything more than you can give." I press my hands against the granite surface. "I like you. I like talking to you and having sex with you. If you want this to be a one-night-plus-the-next-day thing, that's fine. But I'd rather have more of this—keep texting, keep sleeping with each other."

Natalie stops rinsing long enough to actually look at me. "I really can't offer you anything more than a casual thing."

"And I'm really not asking you for anything more than that." I believe it when I say it, but as the words come out, they feel like a lie—not so much to her as to myself.

I shove the thought down, grab her wrist, and tug it until she steps around the dishwasher to me. She lays her fists on the counter on either side of me, gently boxing me in.

"We can keep it low-key." I try for levity. "You don't have to text me about *every* burrito bowl."

She fights a laugh, but her small smile breaks through. She's back to the way she's been with me all day, walls that slammed up coming back down just as suddenly.

She rests her chin on the top of my head. "I'm sorry, I was being shitty."

"Mm-hmm," I respond, tilting my head and planting a little kiss behind her ear.

She grabs me by my hips and lifts me onto the kitchen counter, stepping between my widened knees. I wrap my arms around her neck and she kisses me, just once, warm and wet.

"You can tell me to leave again, but say it nicely this time." I hold her gaze. "So we can hang out again sometime soon."

"I have an early practice tomorrow morning, so I would prefer to spend the night alone." Her hands grip my waist, and she presses a kiss to my cheek, sweet as anything. "I'll text you tomorrow night?"

I've done exactly what I meant to do, I think. I walked her back from the ledge of ghosting me, made sure that we held on to this. I kiss her again, pushing down the feeling that there's something empty at the core, a hollowness that wasn't there before. I tell myself this is fine, that this is enough. I'm an excellent fucking liar, and I'm willing to live with it, as long as I can blanket it in the satisfaction that I'm giving Natalie what she needs.

XIV

On Sunday, I watch the Dallas Wings lose to the Aces. Later that night, Natalie texts me as she promised she would, and I reward her with a mirror selfie of the bruises she sucked onto my breasts.

"Fuckkkkkkkk," she messages back, and it's almost as satisfying as it was to make her come.

On Monday morning, I get into the office early to catch up on everything that happened with the Cougars while I was reassigned, and I'm deep in a research hole and my third cup of coffee when I hear footsteps approaching my desk.

"Call off the search party," Sean shouts. "I found her."

Sean and Casey crowd around my desk.

"Happy Monday!" I say, with bright insincerity.

"So. What were you up to all weekend while you were ignoring our texts?" Casey hovers over me.

"Nothing." I sip from my mug.

"Uh-huh." She looks at Sean pointedly.

I glance between my friends, and I know it's time, like it or not. "Bar after work?"

"Damn right," Casey says as I wave her out of my airspace.

Before lunch, I drive over to the Cougars training camp, and though this is routine, something feels off in a way I don't know how to define.

I'm wearing my usual disappear-into-the-background outfit, and though the clothes themselves aren't uncomfortable, I keep mentally circling back to them. As my car slips between lanes, churning along the endless Los Angeles highway, I realize I'm rankling at the idea of obscuring myself, hiding myself in the ways I always have. The way I dress, the way I fold myself up and burrow inside myself, the way I compartmentalize—I act like I'm following rules set in stone from on high. But the only person who made the rules is me, and I'm also the only person who is enforcing them. Maybe I used to need my guidelines, but maybe they have outlived their usefulness. And if they aren't rock-solid, well, there's a chance they're as flimsy as tissue paper, and I could just tear them down. Just thinking the thought makes me feel lighter.

When I pull into the familiar parking lot outside the Cougars' practice arena, I dig into my purse and pull out my makeup bag, where I've stored a few hair ties. I pull my hair up into a high bun, exposing my undercut, putting just a hint of myself on display. I'm instantly more at ease, and a smile comes easy as the security guard checking my press pass at the entrance welcomes me back.

I had hoped that slotting back into my old beat would be like coming home, and it is, but what I didn't expect is that it would be like visiting an old school after graduating, like everything is slightly smaller than you remember it being. The place hasn't changed, but you have.

Outside on the practice green, I sit on the bleachers watching Kyland Green throw passes under the watchful eye of the quarterback coach. Rachel Paulson—an assistant coach and the only female member of the Cougars' coaching team—calls out, "Hey Felix, love the new hair."

"I didn't—" I start, cutting myself off when I realize it's as good as a fresh cut to her. "Thanks."

I can't tell if the feeling in my stomach is happiness or nervousness at being seen. Or both. I realize that maybe this is the first time that Rachel—whose wife also works for the NFL—realizes I am a dyke too. I'm tempted to text Natalie about it, but this feels too heavy for our "keeping it casual" status. I love Casey and Sean, but they're both straight, and I'm not close enough to my lesbian friends to send them something so emotional and abstract. It's lonely to not have anyone to convey this feeling to.

I watch the rest of practice, then introduce myself to Kyland. I've been following him closely, but as a rookie, he only joined practice while I was reassigned. After a few locker room chats with the players I'm closest to, I head back to El Segundo and Bar, where Casey and Sean are already waiting.

"How was work today?" I take a seat next to Sean, putting

him between myself and Casey's more pointed questions, and order a martini from Brody, who knows how I like it.

"Actually"—Sean reaches for a coaster—"I have a question for you about the Lights facility plans—"

"Nope," Casey cuts in. "Work talk can wait. Whatever you're hiding, you better spill immediately." She manages to sound extremely focused on me without breaking eye contact with the TV above her.

Brody sets my drink in front of me, and I slump into it, slurping from the nearly overflowing glass, hoping for some psychosomatic liquid fortification. "I have told a lie to my friend Sean about the origin of a ticket to a basketball game and engaged in sexual acts with a player."

"I knew it!" Casey shouts triumphantly.

Sean manages to look both gleeful and slightly hurt simultaneously. "I take it the friends and family ticket wasn't a gift from a publicist and was in fact a gift from . . . Natalie Czapski?"

"Yes indeed."

"I would've kept your secret," Sean says. "Even from Casey."

"Hey!" Casey hits him lightly on the arm, but her tone is cutting. "How did this even happen?"

I start with the texting, our flirtatious night in Vegas. Casey's expression gets sharper the deeper I get into my explanation. "But I mean, is it just a physical attraction thing only or are you trying to date her?"

"Neither?" I let my eyes drift to the bottles behind the

bar. "I like spending time with her on a personal level, but she's not open to dating, so it's going to stay casual."

Casey knows more than anyone that I have a history of going for women who overpromise and underdeliver, women who will say they don't want anything, then act like I'm the only one they care about for a few weeks, then post a picture of another girl on their Instagram. Variations on a theme. She scowls a little. "This sounds a lot like your thing with Kristen. And your thing with Laura. And the one, what's her name, who cheated on you with Laura."

"Jen," I supply.

"Or fucking Jen," Casey says.

"Fuck *that* Jen," Sean nods, amicably.

"This is not like Kristen, Laura, and Jen," I say, hoping Casey won't follow up by asking how, exactly, Natalie isn't part of my bad pattern, because the only answer I have is that I already like Natalie more than I liked any of my exes. And that isn't a reassuring *private* thought, much less a sentiment that would convince Casey.

"How, exactly, is this not like Kristen, Laura, and Jen?" Casey throws up her hands.

I'm saved by Brody delivering Sean and Casey's beers and breaking up the cadence of the conversation so I don't have to answer.

"It's not that I'm dying for a casual hookup." I clink my half-empty martini glass against Casey and Sean's full pints. "I just like Natalie, and she has expressed what she wants—what she can handle—so I'll give her that."

"But what do *you* want?" Casey narrows her eyes.

"I want exactly this," I lie.

Casey scowls more deeply.

"I guess, isn't that kind of the best-case scenario for you too, ultimately?" Sean is trying to smooth things over, as usual. "I know you're not writing about the Lights anymore and it's not like it's an actual work conflict, but dating a professional athlete—it'd be complicated even if you weren't a reporter."

This is something we all know as sportswriters, that the "wives and girlfriends" are a part of the story. WAG culture became part of the sports narrative well before athletes were dating famous influencers or Taylor Swift. And if there's one thing they know I despise, it's stepping into any kind of spotlight.

Casey shakes her head, exasperated. "Sean! How is it a good idea for our friend to date yet another woman who doesn't wanna make space in her life for her?"

"How is it a good idea for my friends to decide what's best for me instead of me deciding for myself?" I snap back maybe a little too roughly.

"The girls are fighting," Sean does his singsong voice, still trying to break the tension.

"It's going to be fine." I look toward the TV even though I don't know what game is on.

"How can you possibly know that?" Casey asks.

"Through the force of my will," I say at the screen.

"I hope you're right. I hope it's fun and cool and no hurt feelings." It's clear Casey believes with her whole soul that it will not be like that.

"And good sex." Sean raises a hand.

"Already got that one covered." I shoot finger guns at him, and he high-fives me.

"Well, if it all goes to shit, you better come crying to me, so I can say 'I told you so.'" Casey returns to her beer.

"I promise."

My phone, resting face-up on the bar top, lights up with a text from Natalie: "Can you come to the game on Thursday?"

Casey and Sean see it before I can hide my screen or my grin.

"This is exactly what I want." I try to keep my voice as light as possible. "Good tickets to a basketball game."

"I'm free," I text back, performing for my friends, and I catch Casey smiling despite herself.

XV

Over the next two weeks, I'm busy. Not too busy to worry about the way the NFL no longer feels like my softest sweatshirt and instead feels like an itchy wool sweater. Not too busy to tie myself up in knots every time I want to text Natalie, worried that the correspondence that was previously second nature now somehow violates the terms of our agreement to keep it casual. But busy enough that I don't have time to let my concerns overwhelm me.

I spend my mornings at Cougars practice and my afternoons at the office, banging out a few standard preseason stories and updating my notes document. Most evenings, I'm at home, catching up on the nonfiction books I promised myself I would read before NFL opening day.

The first Lights game I go to post-sleepover, I still manage to stay under everyone's radar. I sit next to the teenage brothers of one of the centers, because they're the family members least likely to strike up a conversation.

After, in the worn-down VIP lounge, Natalie informs me that the hot water is out at her place, and without overthinking it, I drive us to mine. Natalie looks big and pretty and a little out of place in my low-ceilinged bungalow, but she thumbs at my books with genuine curiosity and proclaims her undying love for my oversize couch. It's too much like we're going through the motions of getting to know each other in a girlfriendy way, so to chase away that feeling, I pull her on top of me onto the cushions. She kisses me, her leg wedged between my thighs. It's enough to get me worked up but not enough to get me off, and she teases me like that—"Oh, you want more?"—for what seems like forever, until I'm begging her to take off my clothes and fuck me fully.

I wake up too early to Natalie's alarm in my bed, with her body draped over mine like a blanket and her forehead pressed into my shoulder, like a gigantic cat hiding its face from the light.

"Fucking helllllll," she rasps, pawing at her phone to turn off the sound. "Early practice."

She squeezes me once, almost too tight, then detangles from me and hoists herself out of bed. Yawning, I follow her.

"You don't have to get up," she says, retrieving her boxer briefs from where they fell the night before, half under my bed.

"It's fine. I won't be able to fall asleep again anyway."

In my kitchen, I put water in my Mr. Coffee machine

and grind beans while Natalie distracts me, tugging at me until I kiss her.

But she also calls a car, and it comes faster than either of us expects. She's gone before the coffee finishes brewing, and I'm left with a full pot to drink alone.

At the next game, when I slip out of my seat at halftime to gorge on the mini chicken tinga tacos I've developed an obsession with, I hear a voice to my left say, "Hey!" I turn from my plate and recognize the woman from the first night in the lounge.

"Romy Jones. I'm Olivia's wife," she says, reaching out a hand, and her electric blue nails match both her eyeshadow and her woven Bottega Veneta bag. It doesn't seem to me like she has been in LA long enough to switch up her entire style to match Lights colors, but one thing I've learned: Never underestimate a WAG. Her gaze is unwavering and piercing.

"Hey, I'm Felix." I hear my reluctance. I'm not sure how to navigate this and my own precarity. How do I mix with the team's friends and family as someone whose place here is both temporary and complicated, without coming off as cold at best?

"Nice to meet you, Felix," Romy says, as warm as I am chilly, as she waves over a young trans guy. "This is Jay."

Jay looks impossibly cool in a khaki suit, and when he's

close enough to shake my hand, I see the print on his tie is a repeated "15," Jada Jackson's number.

Jay hands Romy a beer, and she somehow manages to take a sip without breaking eye contact with me. "So you're seeing Natalie?" She forces her tone to be casual, but her eyes betray her deep curiosity.

"We're friends." I smile, and my forced brightness makes me cringe. Why am I acting like these are gotcha questions?

"I've seen you here a few times. Natalie doesn't usually have her 'friends' come so often." Jay somehow makes the scare quotes around the word *friends* audible without an accompanying gesture.

I shrug. "Well, I'll choose to be flattered."

"You should be." Romy emphasizes each word with what I am learning might be hallmark intensity.

Jay taps Romy on the shoulder and points to one of the screens on the wall that's playing a live stream of the court. A countdown clock shows that there are only about thirty seconds left of halftime.

"We're going to head back to our seats, but we just wanted to let you know you're welcome to sit with us," Romy says, and Jay nods in agreement.

"Thanks. I . . ." I nod. "That's really kind of you."

We say our goodbyes, and I order an old-fashioned as the lounge empties out. I feel a sliver of unease. I think of myself as on the fringes of this world, in a category all my own, someone who couldn't possibly have a genuine rooting interest, but in Romy and Jay's eyes, I'm one of them, invited to join an exclusive club. They want to make me feel welcome in a group I didn't realize I belonged in. If Natalie invites me to another game, I could sit with them without any of the WAGs batting an eye—but I have no idea how Natalie would feel about it. I have no idea how *I* would feel about it. For what seems like the millionth time in the past two weeks, the ground under my feet, which I once thought was concrete, feels like sand.

I return to my original chair in teen-boy row, and I repress any further overthinking with overzealous attention to every play of the game. The Lights win by twelve anticlimactically, and I'm on edge until I'm in the passenger seat of Natalie's too-big Range Rover and she says, "Let's go to your place."

I exhale at the prospect of Natalie and me cozied up on my big couch, the creature comfort I need. I think I'm hiding how much the conversation with Romy rattled me until Natalie takes her right hand off the steering wheel and squeezes my knee.

"What's up, babe?" Her voice is light, casual as anything.

"What makes you think something is up?"

"You're being quiet." She circles her thumb on my leg.

"I'm always quiet," I respond, a little peevishly. I know I'm not getting away with this. I can't decide what I hate more: that I always try to hide my emotions or the people who won't let me.

Natalie stops at a red light and gives me a look like, *Be so fucking for real for a second.*

I sigh, caught out. I pull her hand off my knee and

into my lap, lacing my fingers with hers instead. She squeezes my palm.

"Romy invited me to sit with the WAGs tonight." I watch her face, and when I don't see a reaction, I add uneasily, "I met her and Jay."

Natalie's posture stiffens, and her hand in mine goes limp. I instantly realize my miscalculation—that Natalie might interpret this as me attempting to raise stakes between us. I should've had this conversation with Sean, or Casey, people who don't have their own skin in the game.

"It's not applicable to our situation." My words are rushing from my lips now. "And yes it's nice she was nice to me, but it makes me uncomfortable to be looped in with the WAGs, like my existence could be defined by who I'm dating. To say nothing of the fact that I'm a sports reporter. And I also feel sort of shitty reacting this way because I know all of them have big, interesting lives and do their own things, and I don't want it to seem like I'm rejecting their world—them—out of some kind of disrespect. Like, obviously there's nothing *wrong* with people showing up for their partners?"

Natalie's shoulders drop, and her fingers tighten in mine again.

"Yeah, fuck, I'm sorry, I thought you were saying . . ." She trails off.

I guessed right: She thought I was trying to start a conversation about being her girlfriend. I feel a pang of sympathy for the women who have very possibly been in my place, in this passenger seat, before, asking for something they weren't going to get. I feel a pang of sympathy for myself. As much as I like Natalie, I am never going to get to hold on to her. I grip her hand more firmly, as if I fear her slipping through my fingers here and now.

"Anyway," Natalie is still talking, "yeah, I love all of our WAGs and how they show up for us. And I also understand wanting to be in control of how you're perceived."

"Exactly." There's a tightness in my throat when I say it.

"I think about this all the time actually, how to share who I am with people who don't know me but are rooting for me, or for the Lights. It's not easy to figure out how much to show and when to show it."

Natalie's not expressing anything revolutionary, but it's one of those moments when something mundane slips into something almost profound. *It's not easy to figure out how much to show and when to show it.* This is the calculation I run a thousand times a day. When Casey asks me to do an on-camera interview. When Romy extended her invitation. It's like the edges of my own story blur and become indistinct to me, and my own understanding of myself starts to break down. If I say yes to this small thing, will I be perceived as I want to be? Will I give too much of myself, or the wrong parts?

I look out the windshield at the road, blinking fast. "It's impossible, I know, but I want to be the one who decides how other people see me."

Natalie nods vigorously. "That's exactly it."

It's a comment that should make me feel closer to her, and it does, in that it's obvious to me that this is something we're both struggling with, a point of connection between us. But it also reminds me that no matter how well she can read my feelings or how well we understand each other, my connection with Natalie is always going to be stunted, limited by the boundaries she's putting in place. I push the thoughts out of my mind. If I don't, they'll overtake the entire evening, and more than anything, I need a release.

XVI

When we get to my house, Natalie barely waits for me to toe off my shoes before hustling me into the bedroom, undressing me and then herself and arranging our bodies on the bed so that, despite our height difference, we can lie on our sides and make out. There's so much skin against skin that I'm almost oversensitive, nerve endings zinging, and I can't keep my hands still, wanting to touch her back, her hips, her neck, her ass, all at once. I slip a hand down her thigh and nudge until her knee bends and she throws the leg over me, pinning me between all that skin and my mattress.

Natalie breaks our kiss and murmurs, "I like talking to you."

"This activity would not necessarily be described as talking," I say.

Natalie chuckles, a low rumble.

"I like talking to you," she says again, ducking her head to kiss me on one collarbone. "I like spending time with you." She kisses the other collarbone. "I like fucking you too."

I'm too hot, too wet, too ready to blurt out some real feelingsy shit. How am I supposed to respond to that while "keeping it casual"? How does Natalie *fucking* Czapski think this type of talk fits in with her no-girlfriends rule?

Natalie saves me—and herself, really—by moving on from the sweet nothings portion of the evening and slipping two of my fingers into her mouth, sucking until they're wet, then guiding them into herself. She does the same to her own fingers, and I watch her, my jaw hanging open, as she gets herself ready to fuck me. When we're inside of each other, we move our hands how we know the other likes it and then kiss wetly through our orgasms, and it's the sweetest sex we've ever had.

She lies on her back and I drape my body over hers, nestling my head into her shoulder and licking at her salty skin.

"Pervert," she chuckles.

"You smell good. You taste good." Luckily, I've figured out how to speak to her and keep my tender little feelings to myself.

She kisses the side of my face, right by my ear. "You too. Do you mind if I stay the night?"

"Please."

The next morning, we walk to the coffee shop near my apartment to pick up cold brews and breakfast burritos. We eat standing up at my kitchen counter, just like I always do, like she's slipping herself into my usual routine. And then she just stays.

"I have to work," I tell her reluctantly as I clean up our wrappers.

"Cool if I just lay around?" she asks, and again I feel the clash between her request to keep it casual and the way she acts. But ultimately, I'd rather she stay than leave.

"Make yourself at home," I say as she wanders over to one of my bookcases.

I sit down at the small wooden table shoved in a corner of my living room. It is supposed to be for dining but is always too covered with papers and books to be functional as anything other than a desk. Natalie crouches in front of one of the shelves and pulls out a copy of *The Golden Compass.*

"Have you ever read it?" I ask. "It was my favorite fantasy novel when I was a kid."

"Today's the day." She flops onto my couch, puts a pillow under her head, and cracks open the spine.

And then for hours we just sit quietly together. Pages flip and ruffle. I build out components that will likely go into my story about the Cougars' first game, and Natalie seems to develop a sixth sense for the right moments to interject. When I get up to refill my water, she calls out, "Lyra is so fucking cool, I would've wanted to be her if I read this when I was young," and after a bathroom break, "Please tell me nothing happens to Pan. I won't be able to take it."

When I finish my work, I take a few moments to watch Natalie. She's lost in the book, her eyes darting across the page, her lip between her teeth in deep concentration. Though the animal heat of my desire thrums through me, it's less urgent than the quiet contentment—warmth and calm—that spreads over me, like slipping into a bath.

I really, really like Natalie. Which means I'm in trouble.

I submerge myself in the feeling of how much I like her, then I soak in it for a few moments. I let it into my fingers and brain and bones, into my toenails and hair follicles, into the curves of my shoulders and clavicle. Then I fold it up so small I can't really feel it anymore, and I wonder what I can do with it instead of experiencing it.

On the couch, Natalie finally feels my eyes on her. She closes the novel and smiles at me languidly. "How's the piece coming?"

"I feel good about it."

"Are there any guys in the NFL who are secretly gay?" she asks, waggling an eyebrow.

I shrug. "I don't know if anybody is for sure, but I wouldn't be surprised. Maybe there are fewer gay guys than in a randomized group because they self-select out of the environment, you know? At a certain age, young gay athletes might decide not to pursue football if they'd have to stay in the closet their whole career."

Natalie nods meaningfully. "Sometimes I think about how much it must've sucked for the first group of women in the WNBA. There was a lot of pressure on the lesbians to stay in the closet. And have you seen those pictures of Diana Taurasi at the beginning of her career? In those little dresses they used to make her wear?"

“Oh my god, no, please send me some.” I purse my lips, thinking of my first day back at training camp. “There are a lot of queer women who work in the NFL though. Coaches, athletic trainers.”

“Oh, that’s cool, I didn’t know that.” Natalie’s eyes are on her phone. “Come over here, so I can show you these photos.” She holds out one arm like she wants me to lie on top of her.

“Just a sec.”

I flick open my NFL notes document on my computer and start a new section, “Queer NFL??” Then I close my laptop, go to the couch, and let Natalie wrap herself around me.

On Sunday, Natalie leaves for a long road trip, taking with her my copy of *The Golden Compass* and its sequel, *The Subtle Knife*.

On Monday morning at the office, I start to add things to my “Queer NFL??” notes. At first, all my ramblings read like some embarrassing combination of wishful thinking and a want ad that reads “Dyke NFL fan seeking same.” But there’s a spark of something in there, and I tease it all morning until it’s something real. I delete the question marks—just “Queer NFL” now—and knock on David’s office.

He waves for me to join him, and I jump right into pitching him two features: one about LGBT coaching staff in the NFL, and an LA texture piece about queer football fans watching games at gay sports bars.

"There are gay sports bars?" David barks out with a too-big laugh that borders on a scoff, authentically surprised, and then his cheeks go red and he looks sick, like he knows he shouldn't have responded that way. I've never seen David unmoored, and it makes me feel a queasy secondhand embarrassment. I flick my hand in the air like I'm waving his comment away, hopefully communicating simultaneously that he shouldn't have said it and that I'm not going to hold it against him.

I realize almost immediately that I'm wrong: I *am* going to hold it against him. For my entire adult life—and most of my teenage life too—David has been my North Star, my template for who I want to be as a writer and even as a person. But lately, he has been just a man, as fallible as any other. The David I've idolized is only one portion of a person—someone with good journalistic instincts, an insane talent for sportswriting, and enough bravado to make the most of both. Another part of him is a guy who would reassign the only queer woman who works on his staff to cover the WNBA even though she doesn't know anything about basketball. I don't hate him for it, exactly. I just have to face—probably much later than I should have—that he's not some two-dimensional hero. He is a person with good qualities and bad ones. Like all people. And I have to find a way to be my *own* kind of role model, not just someone who meets whatever needs David has for a reporter.

I keep on with my pitch, more assertive now. "The biggest gay sports bar in LA is Hi Tops. They have locations in West Hollywood and Los Feliz."

I've never gone to Hi Tops to watch a football game, even though I go to sports bars all the time. And gay bars all the time. Over the last forty-eight hours, it's hit me how embarrassing it is that I haven't done anything to create space, or expand or even support the spaces that already exist, for queer football fans. Until now.

David nods. "See what you can find. If you get three good stories, let's run with it."

Back at my desk, I Slack Casey and Sean to tell them I got a soft yes, and Casey sends me a DM:

"I think you should be prepared to talk about your personal reasons for writing this. It would make a big difference for the supplemental coverage on social, and you know how much that can impact story performance."

"Okay. . . ." How many more ellipses would I need to properly communicate my ambivalence?

But then, how much of my discomfort about making myself the face of my stories has been about adhering to David's idea of what a journalist should be? And how much has that been holding me back?

"I'll put together some thoughts." It's all I can manage at this moment. Casey reacts with a thumbs-up emoji, and I know I still have a long way to go.

On the NFL's opening day, I fly to Kansas City to watch the Cougars' offense dominate and their defense fall apart. The Cougars pull off a win, but it's so rough and dirty that it makes me feel demoralized, until I watch a video Natalie took of herself and Louisa tuning into the game. Weesie squints at the television and says in a scandalized tone, "Football just isn't very *pretty*, is it?"

I choke out a laugh and respond, "Tell Weesie I can't wait to teach her how to appreciate America's number-one sport."

After I file, I FaceTime Natalie and we chat through our evening routines, washing our faces, brushing our teeth, getting into bed.

"Do you have a game on the ninth?" Natalie asks as we're both starting to drift off.

"That's a Tuesday? No, they don't have football on Tuesdays."

"We're playing the Fever—will you let me fly you out to Indiana?"

I feel a fluttery, quiet kind of elation. It's the first time Natalie has invited me on the road. I want to read into this, because it feels like an escalation, but I remind myself: Natalie hasn't actually *said* she wants to get more serious. In fact, she's articulated the exact opposite. Just because she's a woman doesn't mean she's different from all the athletes I know, and how many times have football players flown out some girl they DMed on Instagram just to get laid?

But then: I know it's a big game. If the Lights win, they will clinch their spot in the playoffs. From both interviews while I was covering the W and our conversations since, I know Natalie—however stupidly—blames herself for the Lights not making the playoffs last season. She's been playing every game since she got back with a single-minded intensity aimed at "fixing" her "mistake."

"Indianapolis . . . so glamorous." I arch my brow.

Natalie shifts on her pillows, puts one arm over her head, and licks her lips. "Do you want me to beg?"

The space low in my stomach pulses with desire. "I do, actually."

"Please, Felix. Come to Indianapolis with me. Please."

Fuck. It should be silly, but somehow Natalie makes Indiana actually sound sexy. "Yes. But only because you asked so nicely."

We hang up, and I'm so riled up it takes an hour to settle down to sleep.

XVII

I ask Natalie to book me a ticket on the same flight that Sean is taking, and he swaps his window seat with someone's middle so we can sit next to each other. Before takeoff, I watch TikToks until the algorithm serves me a video of Natalie walking into a game wearing a baggy scoop-neck T-shirt that shows off most of her clavicle and her chest tattoos. Under her arm, I spot a copy—my copy—of *The Subtle Knife*. I like the TikTok helplessly and then put my phone on airplane mode to spare myself more feelings.

After takeoff, Sean and I press play simultaneously on *2 Fast 2 Furious* and spend most of the flight arguing through an objective quality ranking of the Fast and Furious movies. As we start our descent, Sean brings up the Lights, because he can't help it.

"You know if they win today, and the Mystics lose, the Lights will clinch the playoffs." His voice is quiet, like he's afraid to jinx it.

"Yup, I know." I fiddle with the button on my armrest, trying to return my seat to its full upright position.

"And the Mystics are playing the Liberty, so they're

probably going to lose," Sean adds. There's about a 1 percent chance Sean thinks he's telling me something I don't know. It's far more likely he's trying to coax me into a conversation about Natalie and my wretched emotions—how I feel warmer toward her every day, a fact I'm trying to avoid thinking about much less saying out loud.

"It's almost as if this is a hugely important game," I tease.

"It's almost as if, if you were playing a hugely important game, you'd want your girlfriend to be there." Sean is usually one for subtlety, but not today. I try to convince myself the pressure between my ears is entirely because of the plane and not because of what Sean is saying.

"It's almost as if . . . you'd want someone to cheer you on even if said person wasn't your girlfriend but instead the beautiful, accomplished woman you've been having a fun, casual fling with." I bat my eyes at him.

Sean shrugs, not willing to push me any further.

The wheels of the plane hit the tarmac and we bounce in unison. "Too bad you can't join me in the good seats," I say, like I've won.

The game is an exercise in acute sports suffering. The Fever's spot in the playoffs is guaranteed, but if they win, they'll be the fourth seed and will start their playoff run with a home game. It's an advantage that matters enough that the Fever's best players are not only playing long minutes but are also visibly hungry for the victory. I ride through a roller coaster of elation and defeat as the Lights and the Fever play four tight quarters, the lead switching a dizzying twenty-one times.

Though I'm in my usual position next to the younger siblings, I see Romy and the other WAGs glance my way more than once. Jay, wearing another immaculately cut suit, waves, and I wave back, trying to communicate the complicated message of "I'm not going over there, but it has nothing to do with you!" with the simplest of gestures.

With 5.5 seconds left in the game, the Lights are down one point. Natalie finds an opening near the three-point line. She steps back. She shoots. The ball falls cleanly, softly through the hoop. I scream with the rest of the Lights' friends and family section as the buzzer sounds and the Lights officially win.

On the court, Natalie drops into a deep squat, puts her head in her hands, and cries.

When Jay, Romy, and the other WAGs join the players on the court, I hang back, hovering near the courtside seats, out of the frame of the cameras that circle the players. I watch as Natalie clutches at her teammates. When she spots me, she jogs over and I note that the lenses don't follow. She wraps her arms around me, burying her face into my shoulder. When she pulls away, I reach my thumb up to her cheek, brushing away the remnants of her happy tears. I want to suck my thumb into my mouth and taste her salt.

"Congratulations babe, you fucking did it," I say.

"I can't believe it." Her breathing is heavy, like she's still collecting herself.

For a few perfect seconds, I forget everything except the warm press of her body. Then a flash of light goes off somewhere to the side—a camera, or a hundred—and the old panic blooms in my chest. I pull back sharply, stumbling a little and turning my face away. When I glance back at Natalie, she's grinning like nothing's wrong. I force myself to smile too, but the awareness of all those lenses, those eyes, doesn't leave me.

When Ashley pulls Natalie away for the presser, she raises her eyebrows at me knowingly, and even though her response is friendly—charmed, even—it's the last straw. Instead of going to the locker room with the other friends and family, I head back to the hotel and message Natalie to let her know. I change from my blue T-shirt into something sexier, and just as I pull out my phone to follow up with Natalie, it lights up with a text from her.

Natalie: "Everyone is going to Invy Nightclub, and I've gotta go for one drink. But do you want to meet for dinner in like an hour?"

Me: "There's an Italian place."

Natalie: "I'm there."

An hour later, I'm waiting in the booth of an old-school red-sauce restaurant I always eat at when the Cougars are playing the Indianapolis Colts, fending off Sean's texts ("I assume you're too busy with your not-girlfriend to grab a nightcap with me??" "How would you feel if you flew your not-girlfriend all the way to Indianapolis and she ditched you for a coworker?" "How did I get demoted from friend to coworker??") and tugging at the edges of the checkered tablecloth, nervous that after a big win and partying at the club, a dinner for two won't rise to the occasion.

The thought falls out of my head when I feel Natalie's arms wrap around my shoulders from behind and her lips drop a kiss on my crown. "Thanks for waiting, babe," she says quietly in my ear.

She sits and immediately digs into the bread basket, shaking more parm into the olive oil dish, eating like a famished person. With her mouth half full, she starts taking me through the last five minutes of the game: everything she was thinking, what it felt like to hit the three-pointer, how hard she's been working to be a real three-and-D player. All I can think about is the first time we talked during All-Star weekend, when she barely looked at me, evaded my questions, and always paused before she spoke. How much I wanted to crack her open like an egg, and how I never in my wildest dreams could've imagined how good this casual intimacy would feel.

A waiter delivers my fettuccine Alfredo and her rigatoni Bolognese, and Natalie reaches her fork across the table to steal a bite of my dish like she knows I won't mind, that I welcome sharing.

"Okay, I don't wanna step all over your moment"—I twirl my noodles—"but I do have a little work update. That you inspired, in fact."

I share my progress on my feature about queerer spaces in the NFL while she makes quick work of her dinner. Her responses and follow-ups—"Oh, someone said that women's sports bar, Sports Bra, is opening here!"—make my blood buzz like I've had twice as much wine as I've actually consumed. For a whole pasta course, it feels like maybe something bigger is happening here than a casual hookup.

A nasty little voice in my head reminds me that this wouldn't be the first time I've misread signals from somebody I was sleeping with, but tonight, I push down that voice and let myself bask in what I'm actually experiencing: our connection.

We split the tiramisu and Natalie insists on paying—"Nah, I'm treating you," she says when I reach for my wallet. We get an Uber back to the hotel, her hand above my knee like it had been at the poker table in Vegas. When we're alone in the elevator, I'm still dwelling on the gesture. "Do you like touching me like that?" I pull her palm onto my leg, high up on my inner thigh.

She looks a little sheepish. "Yeah, don't you like it too?"

"Yeah, I really like it. And I like hearing you say it."

"Fucking journalists," she jokes, "always wanting me to yap."

In the hotel room, she yaps. She takes off my shirt and tells me how much she likes the way my tits look and how sensitive they are and how hard my nipples get when she sucks them into her mouth. She says she likes it when I rub myself over my pants, using the seam of my jeans to apply pressure to my clit. She says she likes the way my pussy smells and thinks it's fun to tease both of us by licking me over my lacy little underwear. We're both steaming and throbbing and I'm straddling her on the bed when she pulls away just enough to whisper in my ear, "Do you like getting fucked with a strap-on?"

"Yeah, yes, I mean—oh my god, did you bring a strap in your carry-on?"

She smiles that big cocky smile and nods slowly. She moves my right hand so I'm touching myself and says, "Keep going, I'll be right back."

I do as she says, but I move to my knees so I can watch her buckle the harness around her thighs and slick up the silicone dildo with some expensive-looking lube. She keeps her eyes on me, lashes fluttering, and I unravel, opening up to her, trusting her to take care of me.

Natalie arranges us on the bed so we're back in that position I've learned she loves, her propped against the headboard and me bracketing her thighs. I let her guide the dildo inside me, gently nudging her and shifting my hips to get the angle right, until she's bottomed out and I feel that delicious full feeling.

"I want to watch you move," she says, and I brace my arm above her as I fuck myself and press my fingers to my clit. She stares unblinkingly, her gaze hot.

I huff out hot little breaths as the fire builds inside me. Natalie bites hard on my earlobe and asks, "Are you close?"

"Uh-huh, yes." My voice is embarrassingly high.

She knocks my hand away from my clit and presses against it with her fingers, and it's like all her watching was really studying—like she was dissecting fucking game film—because she knows exactly how to touch me.

I want to say clichéd things, scream *Please don't stop*, but

I don't have to because she doesn't, and my orgasm hits like an electric shock. I kiss her for languid, frothy minutes and run my nails down her arms as she slips her fingers under the leather of the strap and moves them until she comes as well.

After, I nudge her into a reversal of our usual positions, so I'm lying on my back and her head is pillowed on my shoulder and sternum, one arm under me and the other softly tracing my ribcage and the soft swell of my stomach.

"Did you like that?" she asks, softly.

"I did."

"What did you like about it?"

"Fucking journalists," I say, "always wanting me to yap."

She pinches my nipple hard in retribution and I shout and laugh, rubbing at the ache.

"If you keep doing that I'm going to need to come again." I nuzzle my head against hers.

"Tell me what you like about it." Her hands return to their gentle touches on my skin, but her tone is insistent.

"I like how you watch me, study me. How good you are at making me come." I shrug as much as I can under the weight of her body. "It makes me feel close to the person I'm fucking. Sleeping with."

"Making looooove to." She delivers the line in a sing-song voice, but then goes serious. "Yeah I get it. That's what I like about it too. It makes me feel really close."

I kiss her head, taking in the smell of flowers and rain, the frizz of her sex-mussed French braids. I absently wish I knew how to style hair, just so I could redo them for her.

Natalie lifts herself off my body and looks at me, eyes big and intense, with an expression I've never seen from her. It makes me want to blink my vision clear, sit up straight, and restart my postcoital brain.

"Come here." I want to kiss her, but more than that, I want to lie with her weight on me and stay in the feeling for as long as I can.

Remember this, I tell myself. *No matter what happens, remember what it feels like when Natalie is holding you like she wants to keep you.*

XVIII

I fly from Indianapolis to Philadelphia, where the Cougars win against the Eagles in a sunny Sunday day game so pretty it's hard to keep a neutral tone when I'm writing my gamer. David's book says that journalists' language should be neither adverbial nor flowery; no matter what you see on the field, your piece should be an accounting of facts. But what David thinks doesn't matter quite as much to me anymore.

I add a few details about the beauty of the game, nothing unreportorial, just attempts to capture the feeling of watching a sport that I love. I leave in a few modifiers I might have cut before. I file the story and walk from Lincoln Financial Field back to my hotel, passing packs of drunk Eagles fans singing their Philadelphia sports song to the tune of "Oh My Darling, Clementine," the lyrics defensive and insane: *"We're from Philly, fucking Philly, no one likes us, we don't care!!"*

I grab my bags and catch a train to New York City, where the Lights have their first playoff game against the Liberty. Technically, I'm also here to work—I managed to finagle it so my reporting trip for my story about queer NFL fans and women's sports bars aligns with Natalie's first playoff game—so the *Chronicle* has booked me a hotel room at a depressing Marriott in a depressing part of Downtown Brooklyn. I take advantage of virtual check-in to make it seem like I'm staying there instead of heading straight to the Moxy Williamsburg hotel where Natalie is staying.

When I arrive, Natalie is out, but she's already made herself at home: The bathroom sink is crowded with her toiletries, her clothes are piled on one side of the bed, and she's stacked all the books in the *Golden Compass* series that I lent her on the nightstand. They look more worn-in since I last saw them, dog-eared and creased like they've been read by someone who loves them. We're both the kind of people who throw our belongings all over hotel rooms instead of keeping them packed tight in overstuffed suitcases, and I love that it feels like permission to be myself in this room I'm sharing with her.

I strip off my button-down and toss it into the corner, and as I dig through my bag for a black tank top, I spot one of Natalie's big white T-shirts slung over the back of the desk chair. I grab it, and the cotton is as soft as I remember from the times I pulled this shirt, or an identical one, over Natalie's head. I smell it for reasons that are only slightly horny and inhale mostly detergent, only a whiff of Natalie's petrichor and her salty, peppery sweat.

I yank it on, grab my huge tote bag filled with all my writing supplies, and leave the hotel. I schlep down to the

Lower East Side to interview the owners of a women's sports bar called Wilka's and then back to Clinton Hill to visit a new queer bar, which is already filling up with Liberty fans ninety minutes before tip-off.

When I find a seat, I'm surprised but elated to see a bartender in a Lights T-shirt and I flag her over, explaining that I'm visiting from LA. She pours me a glass of orange wine and tells me that her wife got a great job in New York, so she was forced to move away from "Los Angeles, a perfect place." When she turns her back to swipe my card, I see she's wearing "Czapski" across her back.

As I sip my drink, I text Casey about the bar, and predictably, she tries to get me to commit to taping a video for social about the story. My first instinct is to say no—to keep the comfortable shield of invisibility in place. I stare down at my phone, my thumb hovering.

Across the room, a group of fans in Liberty jerseys are laughing, their faces painted in team colors, completely unselfconscious. A couple in matching Lights sweatshirts snaps a selfie, kissing quick and easy. I think about how long it took me to realize I could write queer stories about the NFL. About how Natalie moves through the world—not making a show of who she is, but not hiding it either. About how conspicuousness makes it easier for the next person.

I pitch Casey a compromise: a video tour of gay and women's sports bars across the country. I agree to stand in front of Casey's Canon 5D long enough to say "Hi, my name is Jennifer Felix, NFL reporter for the *LA*

Chronicle" and to capture footage in the bars I visit and record voice-over.

Casey agrees by sending me a wall of about fifty eye-roll emoji. I snort into the dregs of my wine.

"Did I not say I would be on camera!!" I thumb back. "Live in the good side of this, please."

She sends me more eye-roll emoji and the middle finger. Then a big red heart. Then a GIF of Sara Bareilles mouthing, "*I wanna see you be brave!*"

"Another?" The bartender has the bottle ready.

"Can you close me out, actually?"

"Where are you running off to?"

"I have tickets to the game." I check the time on the TV.

"Lucky!"

"Perks of the job," I lie.

At Barclays Center, the pregame excitement sinks into my bones. I take my place at the edge of the two-row friends and family section, just behind the far end of the visitor's bench, and wave at Romy and Jay, grateful that they seem content to let me do my own thing. I nod at the seatmates I have come to recognize: Louisa's six-year-old nephew, who is always with a babysitter and likes to stick his tongue out at the refs. Jada Jackson's twin brother, who spends every game twisting a towel nervously in his hands and screaming "THAT'S A FOUL" at plays that aren't fouls.

As the lights come down, the Liberty's mascot, Ellie

the Elephant, dances to a Missy Elliott song, and fans of both teams lose their minds. An uneventful five minutes into the first quarter, someone plops into the empty seat at my right. My eyes are on the court, and I don't realize who it is until a voice says "Hey girl" familiarly.

"Louisa! What are you doing up here?" It's the first time we're seeing each other in person since we met at All Stars, even though I've been getting dispatches from her through Natalie ever since.

Louisa holds up her wrist, wrapped in a bandage.

"You're not on the bench, though?"

"I had to step away for a quick breather. I hate watching and not being able to do anything."

"You should tell your teammates to score more baskets."

Weesie smirks.

I hear the Lights' coach call for a time-out and gesture at Louisa to come back.

"I'll deliver your message," she says, stepping over the chairs and sliding into the huddle.

When the play starts again, Louisa sits on the far end of the bench right in front of me. Jada makes a stunning pass, and I jump to my feet at the same time as Louisa does. She glances over her shoulder and we shout with equal levels of elation. I don't worry anymore about how I'm supposed to act.

The first quarter stays low-scoring and mostly uneventful. The Liberty are clogging up the paint and forcing the Lights to take difficult three-pointers that they just aren't hitting. But on the other end of the court, Natalie is holding the defense on her shoulders, with two big blocks in the first five minutes. No one's shots are landing, and all the players look frustrated.

I spot Charlie Blake and Maya McPherson sitting courtside, Maya wearing a Liberty jersey and Charlie in an "Everyone Watches Women's Sports" T-shirt under a thick, expensive-looking cardigan. Despite myself, I'm a little starstruck. I was a big Mischief fan when I was in middle school, and like a lot of queer women, Charlie was always my favorite. Maya is beautiful, of course, but she carries herself as if to deflect attention—just as much as Charlie absorbs it. But when the word *serene* pops into my head, she stands up and shouts "Oh fucking COME ON" at a ref who fails to call what is an obvious foul against the Liberty.

The second quarter opens with the Lights going on a ten-point run, and my section of the arena starts to hum. They're playing unselfish basketball—not rushing to take good shots, instead waiting for *great* ones. When Natalie sinks a three that brings the Lights to a thirteen-point lead, Louisa and I both bolt up and scream, thrusting our fingers in the air. The Liberty coach calls a time-out, trying to kill the Lights' momentum before it buries them.

"This shouldn't be happening." Louisa's eyes are wide as she takes her seat.

"I mean, holding their own against the Liberty would be big enough, but a run like this is—it's the kind of momentum swing that changes the whole narrative of the series." I'm talking fast, buzzing.

Louisa laughs, a kindhearted scoff.

"What?" I ask.

"You really sounded like a journalist just then."

I realize then how long it's been since I've actively watched a sporting event with someone who isn't taking notes, searching for the story.

Louisa seems to realize I'm not sure how to respond. "Not like it's a bad thing."

"No, I get it. I mean, it's been a long time since I've experienced games just as a fan."

"Shame." Louisa gives me a wink. "I know Nat appreciates you coming through."

"Oh well, yeah, of course, obviously," I stammer, trying to land on a tone that doesn't reveal too much. "I'm glad to be here. For her. The team."

"It's great to see." Louisa's eyes are on the court now, and so are mine. I welcome the opportunity to back away from the landmines that the conversation presents.

"You've had a strong season." It's as true as it is unrevealing.

"I mean that it's great to see you and Nat together." Louisa turns toward me and rests her gaze on my profile.

I press my lips together and hum, noncommittal, but it's meaningful for Natalie's best friend to give us her stamp of approval. And I would guess that she can see that on my face.

As we watch the Liberty try to claw back into the lead, Louisa talks me through the finer points of the possessions. But the Lights have an answer for every one of their baskets.

At halftime, Natalie passes by our seats on the way into the locker room. She high-fives Louisa, then scrunches her nose at me. Her face melts into a sly smile. "Is that my shirt?"

I want to both squirm and preen. Natalie is close enough to touch, so I lean toward her ear the way any friend might in a loud arena. Except I don't feel *friendly* toward Natalie; I feel a deep tenderness that brushes up against words I shouldn't think and feelings I shouldn't have. I want to stay with my emotions in a way I hardly ever do . . . but we're *casual*, and all I have is what is allowed, the sex and desire. And so I shout in her ear, loud but hidden by everyone else's noise, "I wanted to smell you on me all night."

Natalie clasps her hands together and bangs them against her chest, like she's trying to shock her stopped heart back to life. As much as I fight it, the word *love* flits across my mind like a bird too fast to catch—I push it down, but the warmth of it lingers, blooming hot and reckless in my ribcage. I tell myself it's just the wine-and-beer buzz, it's just the adrenaline of the game, but the thought won't die.

"Fuck. I'm not going to be able to *not* think about that during the second half," Natalie purrs. She leans into me like she's going to add something else, but at the last second she presses her mouth to the hinge of my jaw—quick, hidden, scandalous. We're blocked on all sides, and no one could see it, not the cameras, not her teammates. By the time I register what happened, she's already grinning wide enough to split her face and jogging off to the locker room. It was a thirty-second interaction, and I'm dissecting every beat of it. I press my fingers to the place where she kissed me, and it's hard not to feel that if she can kiss me like that, like she can't help it, that her feelings for me might be more than she says, that the word *love* might be floating into her head and striking her as intensely as it struck me. That maybe I'm not alone in this.

At the end of the third quarter, the Lights are still up by eight, and I get a text from Sean: "Holy shit they could actually win this."

From the bench, Natalie twists around and meets my eyes, her smile unguarded and bright. I feel it all the way to my toes.

At the beginning of the fourth quarter, the Liberty play like bats out of hell. Their starting lineup is back on the court together, handling each possession with aggressive determination. A guard on the Liberty, Jemmye La Roux, comes up with a steal, then tears back toward the basket. Natalie's two steps ahead of her, crossing into La Roux's path, taking the charge with her body. It's expected that Natalie might get knocked down, and if a different player were on the defensive maneuver, my eyes would have flicked up to the hoop to see if the Liberty had gotten the points. But because it's Natalie, my eyes stay on her. She tumbles, like a thousand players before her, like she's done a hundred times herself. And I watch as her head bounces off the court.

I imagine I can hear the crack.

The Lights must have gotten the ball back because

there's no one around Natalie as she curls into a fetal position and wraps her arms around her head. The game blunders on, and I vaguely register the clock ticking like nothing happened. It feels obscene. Natalie is hurt, and somehow, the world doesn't stop.

"Natalie's on the ground!" I yell idiotically. No one on the court can hear me, but I'm standing suddenly. Louisa grips my arm, hard enough to hurt. It's been seconds since Natalie fell. Then Louisa is gone. She rushes onto the court as the ref's whistle echoes and the fans scream and hush and then scream again, and the Lights players circle around Natalie. It's like I'm floating, I can't feel my feet in my shoes or my shoes on the ground, but the blood pounds in my ears so loudly it's hard to hear anything else. The world has stopped now, and somehow that's worse.

"Natalie Czapski is holding her head, on the floor underneath the basket," I make out from a broadcast announcer sitting above me.

My heart speeds up and the knot in my chest tightens. All I can do is watch as three members of the Lights' staff help Natalie walk off the court. She disappears into the tunnel, and the game picks back up, as games do. Normally this seems like the only appropriate thing: for the team to keep playing. But with Natalie injured, it feels unthinkable.

Louisa is back by my side, and she pulls me toward the tunnel. And all I can think is *Not this. Not this, not now, not Natalie. Not this.*

XIX

Louisa and I are told to wait outside the medical treatment room, which is deep in the belly of the arena. Eventually, someone brings us chairs. My frantic worry needs an outlet, so I look at my phone, alternately texting with Sean and refreshing the play-by-play section of the WNBA League Pass app. I watch the live game footage as the Liberty go on a fifteen-point run, taking back the lead and holding on to it through the final minutes, winning 95 to 93.

Even though I know I shouldn't, I turn on the highlights. I watch Natalie take the charge and fall to the ground. I watch her head connect with the court. My hand shakes gripping my phone.

"No news at the presser, but they're holding us for an update soon," Sean messages. "Did you hear anything?"

"Still outside the treatment room. Nothing yet."

"Probably a concussion. Not that bad, all things considered." I try to convince myself that he's right. Concussions—injuries in general—are just a part of life for an athlete. Terrible but not uncommon. It shouldn't feel like a bad omen.

A minute later, a member of the Lights' medical staff steps into the hallway and verifies that Sean's guess is right. I go into journalist mode, asking about the severity and recovery. "Grade two, with no significant neurological symptoms—she'll be back on the court in no time," the doctor reports.

I huff out a sigh of relief. "That's great."

But Louisa shakes her head ruefully. "She'll have to sit out game two."

I hadn't considered that. I should have. It's always a concern with the guys in the NFL, whether or not the concussion protocol would keep them on the sidelines, but I hadn't been thinking about Natalie in those terms. I had been thinking like I was her girlfriend, happy she's okay.

"Jennifer, Natalie asked to talk to you alone for a minute," the doctor says.

Louisa and I lock eyes briefly, and she gives me a solemn nod. The doctor holds open the door, ushering me inside.

Natalie is sitting on a hospital bed, looking away from the entrance, one leg sticking out from under the blankets and jiggling in an anxious rhythm. I step toward her, but not too close. She still hasn't moved to look at me.

"Is your headache bad?" I ask. My voice is steady, but my heartbeat is not.

"They gave me some Aspirin," she says without turning her head.

I hover near her bed, my hands tugging on the hem of my T-shirt—her T-shirt—for lack of something better to do. "How are you feeling?"

Natalie finally looks at me. Her face is set hard, no trace of her usual cocky humor, and her braids are frizzy and coming undone. Her eyes are red and glassy like she's been crying. Seeing her state, I reach out a hand, but I don't make contact. It hovers in midair, in purgatory.

"Please don't touch me," she says.

I freeze. I want to believe that she's worried about her own physical state, but I recognize this version of Natalie, the one who ignored me in the back of the limo during All-Star weekend, who refused to give me real answers or look me in the eyes. The first thing Natalie ever did was reject me, and so I know what's about to happen now.

"Whatever we've been doing, it's obviously over." Her delivery is robotic.

I want things to slow down so I have time to process, to respond, to fight back—but she's still talking, moving into horrible logistics shit: "You can stay in the hotel room tonight, but I'm going to find somewhere else to stay."

"It's not." I'm responding to something she said at least thirty seconds ago, trying hard to catch up, like I've been punched in the gut and I'm attempting to stand up before another blow lands. I clear my throat. "It's not obviously over." Despite my effort to sound authoritative, it comes out petulant and desperate. "You can't just end things like this."

"Of course I can." She's weirdly calm, not even looking at me anymore. All of her is still except that leg bouncing on the bed. "It's not your fault. This was incredibly stupid of me. I should've known something like this would happen."

"Natalie . . ." I take a deep breath, readying myself for

the level of honesty it will require to pull us back from the brink. "Just because we've kept the relationship casual, doesn't mean I can cut off my feelings. I'm—"

"You don't get it, Felix," she says sharply, cutting me off before I can get out *I'm falling for you*. It's the strongest version of my emotions that I can express to her, but the words feel flimsy and formless trapped in my mouth. Hardly an antidote to her poison. I know I'm in love with her, and I know I can't say it. And I know how this—dating me, even without real commitment, and ending up in a hospital bed—must feel like confirmation of her worst fear.

"I couldn't stop thinking about you wearing my stupid fucking shirt on the court tonight and I hurt myself again." Natalie clenches her jaw.

"You didn't hurt yourself because you like me, it was just bad luck, bad timing—"

She acts like she can't even hear me.

"Basketball is the most important thing to me, much more important than whatever dumb shit we were doing together."

It stings so badly I can almost feel it physically. "You know this isn't dumb. You can't just throw this away."

"I can do whatever I want, and I will always do what's best for my game." She shakes her head, like I've worn out her patience. "You should leave." When I make no move to go, she shouts, "Hey, Dr. Beech? Can I switch out my visitors now?"

Dr. Beech emerges from some sub-office and looks at me expectantly until I start heading for the door. In the hallway, I brush past Louisa, not wanting to answer whatever questions she might have for me. My eyes prick and burn and blur as I fumble my way through the maze of the arena's back office, as I do my best not to start crying. I try as hard as I can to press down everything I'm feeling, but it's too big to contain with my flimsy little coping mechanisms. I can't think of anyone's stats except Natalie's.

I nearly bump into a staff member, and I stammer out, "Where is the press briefing room?"

They point down a nearby hallway, and I head that way blindly. In the first good luck I've had since Natalie's head thwacked the hard court, the press is being let out just as I arrive, and the first person I see is Sean.

"Hey—" His eyes go wide when he notices my face. "What's wrong?"

"Let's get out of here."

I'm silent for our entire trip back to the Moxy. If I was alone, my headphones would be in, and I would be trying to use Brian Johnson's growly screech in "Thunderstruck" to scrub all the thoughts out of my head. But I suspect that no matter how much classic rock I blast into my eardrums, I won't be able to scour away Natalie.

Natalie, and the truth: that I'm in love with her. The way she turned away from me, how her stare went hard and flat. And worst of all, the pause. That terrible, familiar lull before she spoke, like I wasn't worth answering. Like we hadn't slept tangled together, whispered secrets in the dark. Or worse—like we had done those things, but they didn't matter.

With each traffic light, the pain wells up, too big and raw to hold by myself. The brush of Sean's sleeve against my arm reminds me that I don't have to be alone. He'll let me seethe quietly or break apart loudly, whatever I need. His hand squeezing my shoulder reminds me I have it in me not just to shove my emotions down but to weather them. Watching Natalie avoid her feelings, push them away, go blank—it makes me want to do the opposite, be stronger, not run away from it. I want to be able to—I *know* I'm able to—fall to pieces right here on the sidewalk and still have the strength to put myself back together.

Sean guides me through an automatic door into a hotel lobby, but not the Moxy. He's delivered me back to where I'm supposed to be staying, but he takes me to his room instead of the one I'm sort of checked into. I manage to dash off a text to Natalie, to let her know I'm not staying where my things are, while Sean calls room service and orders us two plates of fries, two Caesar salads, and four martinis. He hands me a pair of sweats and then I almost start crying when I explain that I need a T-shirt too. He shoves Natalie's into the back of the closet where I can't see it and lends me one of his that's big and gray and soft.

"Do you want to watch *Remember the Titans*?" Sean knows me well enough to know I'll want to do anything other than sit with how upset I am.

"Actually, do you mind if I just—" My voice breaks,

and I let the tears spill. I purse my lips and gesture to my own face, twirling two fingers toward my eyes.

"Oh honey, of course," he says, clutching one of my hands while I cry into the other.

Crying isn't something I can do halfway, or in bits and pieces. When I cry, it's big and messy and loud. I hold myself back from the edge unless it really matters, or I can't help myself. This time, it's a little bit of both. I let myself shake and sob until I can barely breathe, until my body aches with crying, until there's nothing left of me but tears and it's time to put myself back together.

By the time our food arrives, I've cried myself dry. While Sean battles with a ketchup bottle, I slurp alcohol out of an underfull glass. The martini is badly made, with flecks of ice floating on the surface, but I'm too wrung out to care. We eat both french fries and salad with our fingers.

"I always told you, babe, you lose them how you get them," Sean says, "as the result of a sports injury."

Despite myself, I snort around a mouthful of romaine and parmesan. "Don't make me laugh when I am so sad and full of Caesar salad."

"Deepest apologies," Sean smirks.

I squeeze his arm gratefully.

XX

The next morning, I wake to the phone ringing shrilly. Sean jerks upright on the other side of the king bed and rips the receiver off the cradle as I moan.

"Oh great," he says, far too perky. "Tell her I'll be right down."

"What's going on?" I mumble as Sean tugs on his jeans and grabs his key card from the nightstand.

"I'll be back, keep sleeping."

But it's too late, and I'm already up. I check myself in the mirror and find that I'm puffy, worse for wear, but not ruined.

Fifteen minutes later, I hear the electronic click of the door opening. Sean comes in holding two big cups of coffee, Casey trailing behind him.

"What are you doing here?" I'm as appreciative as I am incredulous.

"I was in Boston." Casey flings herself onto the bed and knocks me onto my back in a big hug. "It's like a thirty-second drive. Plus, you promised me I could tell you 'I told you so' when Natalie broke your heart."

I chuckle, but it comes out choked. She whispers, "I told you so," in a way that sounds exactly like "I love you."

I've technically done enough reporting for my sports bars story to take a "sick" day, so instead of working, we become hotel goblins. We visit the grab-and-go café in robes and slippers, take over the pool's sauna to sweat out last night's drinks, and wait outside the hotel's sports bar, Rudy's Game Den, at 11:59 a.m. for it to open at noon.

When we're let in, I slide onto a corner barstool and Casey and Sean sit on either side of me. The TVs are all tuned to ESPN, and we immediately clock the intro show for a Yankees game. We scowl in unison.

"Is there anything else on?" Casey asks a bartender in a Yankees hat.

"Corporate doesn't let us change the channel," he lies.

We submit to our fate: Yankees versus Astros.

"Fuck." Sean orders us three martinis.

After five innings, we're still the only people at Rudy's. I'm slumped over the bar, the entire weight of both my physical and emotional being held up by my elbows. Casey is on her phone doing some last-minute edits on a video that needs to go up on the *Chronicle*'s social accounts before noon Pacific. Sean has been letting me get away with baseball-oriented conversation, but as Casey definitively snaps the case of her earbuds shut, I know my time getting off easy is coming to an end.

Casey's eyes are on the TV as usual, but her voice is sharp. "So. What happened?"

"Easy, tiger," Sean says.

"With love and support and care and undying affection, tell us what happened right now."

"I'm sure you'll be shocked to hear that when I told you that I was happy to keep things casual with Natalie? Well, I was fooling myself. Or lying to myself. And once again—" my eyes sting, my voice catches, but I can manage it, stay with the rawness without falling apart or pushing it away—"I fell for someone who told me from the start that they couldn't give me what I needed. I thought being what she needed was enough. It wasn't."

I dump everything out. I recount my fight with Natalie, but because I haven't done a good enough job of keeping my friends updated about the evolving emotional landscape of my relationship, I keep having to double back and dwell on moments in the recent past, when it seemed like Natalie and I were going to weave our lives together instead of coming apart.

Sean responds first. "The fact that Natalie is too scared to deal with what it means to actually be in a relationship with someone, going through the bad times and the good with them, isn't a reflection on your worth as a romantic partner. This is on her, not you."

Before Casey has a chance to chime in to offer what will inevitably be the firm hand that the situation requires, the bartender interrupts us, gesturing at our empty beers. "You guys want another round?"

“Sure.” Sean hates day drinking but knows when the situation calls for it.

“And shots of tequila,” Casey adds, “but not like Cuervo. Good shit.”

We clink our shot glasses together, tap their bottoms gently on the bar, and throw them back. “All right.” I turn to Casey. “Lay it on me. I can take it.”

“Lay what on you?” She seems genuinely confused.

“I’ve gotten my pump-up speech from Sean, and now it’s time for the tough love. Tell me about how I gave my heart to a risky proposition again. I’m ready to hear it.”

Casey scowls. “What am I? Like, the rain on your funeral parade?”

“I didn’t mean . . .” I start as Sean says, “Kind of!” with a laugh.

“We know you do it to take care of us,” I say. “That’s why it’s called ‘tough love’ and not ‘being a bitch.’”

Casey snorts a guffaw but looks helpless too. “Goddamnit, I wasn’t planning on giving you tough love!”

Sean and I both stare at her, dumbstruck.

“I was going to say”—Casey takes a put-upon sip of beer—“that I’m really happy that you took a chance and were bold and brave with your heart. It sounds like you were doing something different this time around. You found someone who was reaching out to you the same as you were reaching out to her. You were building something wonderful, and you were clearly building it together, and I’m proud of you—and frankly jealous—that you didn’t let the bad experiences from your past keep you from something that seemed so good.”

"Fuck." Immediately, my eyes are watering. I sniff and rub at them with my fists like a baby. "This is somehow worse than tough love."

"Sean's right, it's not your fault. Natalie ran scared, and you deserve someone who won't, but I'm glad you tried. That means that next time something like this comes along, maybe you'll have it in you to be bold again, and eventually you'll find somebody who has what it takes. I'm proud of you for letting yourself be seen."

"Thanks," I say tearfully, and she hugs me hard and fierce. We only break apart when the bartender shouts gleefully and our eyes all go to the screen, where two Yankees are running the bases and the Astros infield is fumbling what looks like it should've been an easy double play. We cheer in delight, not exactly for the Yankees but definitely against the Astros, and in a fit of camaraderie, our bartender gives us all high fives.

When the game goes to commercial, Sean clears his throat. "Does there really have to be a next time?"

"What, this was my one shot?" I ask.

"God, no." He swivels on his stool. "But maybe you and Natalie can work it out."

"There wasn't a lot of ambiguity in our conversation." I focus on the coaster in front of me because I really don't want to replay this again.

"I don't know." Sean throws up a hand. "You know what she's like."

I smile, sad. "And what do *you* know about what she's like?"

"I've been paying attention to her too. It's my job now, remember? She can be a little bit reactive." Sean shrugs. "Acts without thinking. She's a basketball player. Two days ago she was falling in love with you—we all know she was—and those feelings don't just drop out of you, even if you are concussed."

"What am I supposed to do?" I sound more angsty than I mean to.

"I don't know," Sean says. "But maybe something, instead of nothing."

Because nothing is what I usually do. Sean doesn't mean it that way, doesn't mean it as a dig, but he's not wrong. I don't step in front of the camera. I follow David's rules for writing instead of making my own. And in my love life, I don't ask the woman I'm dating for what I need; I just give her whatever she wants.

Maybe this thought should fill me with regret, but I feel the opposite of dragged down. If I was doing nothing before, there's a whole lot of something I could start doing now. A realization that cracks the world open.

On the bar, my phone buzzes. I turn it over to see "Maybe: Weesie."

Casey, nosy, reads over my shoulder. "Like, Louisa Bozley?"

I shrug, then unlock my phone and read the text out loud: "Hey Felix, this is Weesie. I stole your number from Nat's phone. Can I call you in a sec?"

I glance at my friends for some guidance, but they are making me do this myself. I write Louisa back, grab my beer, and head to the hotel room to take the call. When the FaceTime connects, I realize she's calling me from the Moxy. The fabric headboard in her background is the same as in the room Natalie and I were supposed to share.

"Natalie is a fucking idiot for breaking up with you," she says without preamble.

"I can't force her to be my girlfriend." I make myself look into the phone's camera instead of masking how miserable I am.

Louisa lets out a long sigh. "Look. Natty doesn't believe there are things that just *happen*; she believes in cause and effect. She also believes there are no problems she can't fix. So when something occurs that she doesn't like, she finds the cause and then fixes the problem." She sighs again, heavier this time. "Did she tell you what happened with her and Alli?"

"That Alli said something on the court that distracted her, and that's why she tore her ACL."

"Well, that's not really what went down."

My stomach drops. I press my lips together hard, not quite sure yet how I want to take that. "Okay."

"Nat and Alli were only on the court together for no more than thirty seconds. They didn't guard each other; they barely interacted. Personally, I don't think Alli said anything to her on the court that day, distracting or benign." Louisa closes her eyes for a long beat, and I can see the loving frustration in the gesture—not dissimilar to the way Casey can get with me. "I don't think Natalie was lying, at least not intentionally. She's trying to make sense of something terrible that happened to her, that is ultimately senseless. She latched on to Alli as a reason because she couldn't—she still can't—face that idea that she wasn't in control of something that happened to her."

I dig my fingernails into my palms and shake my head. The space under my ribs that once pulsed with my desire for Natalie now aches instead.

For all of our differences, there are places where Natalie and I overlap. Louisa's insights hit me like I'm looking in a mirror and seeing my own reflection for the first time.

Athletes have to give up so much autonomy over so many aspects of their lives. They never know when they might be traded, can't predict when they'll go on a hot streak. So they scramble to control what can't be controlled. Baseball players clutch their superstitions, hockey players won't cut their hair. Natalie refuses to date.

I meet other people's needs instead of addressing my own. The thing I'm trying to control is my own vulnerability, because being vulnerable also means being exposed to pain. Until now, I hadn't been able to see how much avoiding hurt meant I also wasn't giving myself the opportunity to feel joy, and pleasure.

"I don't know what to do with that," I say.

"You don't have to do anything with it if you don't want to," she says gently. "But I thought you deserved some context—some perspective."

"Thanks." I take a breath, and before I can talk myself out of it, I continue. "I fell for her. I'm in love with her."

I curl up on the bed, not caring how pathetic I must

look to Louisa on FaceTime, wallowing in the fetal position, gripping a bottle of Budweiser at 3 p.m.

"I can't tell either of you what to do, but I hope she pulls her head out of her ass." Then Louisa takes pity on me and switches to talk of logistics, how she took my bags out of Natalie's room last night and left them with the front desk for me to pick up.

When I hang up, I know I should go meet Casey and Sean back at the bar, but it takes me a while to move.

XXI

"Felix, do you have a moment? We want to talk to you about a story."

Rachel, the Cougars' assistant coach, interrupts my copyediting daze. The postgame presser ended fifteen minutes ago, and most of the other journalists have already filed their stories and headed home. I'm being, perhaps, obsessive about my copy—mainly because it's been less than forty-eight hours since Natalie's concussion, and the only thing that keeps me from thinking about her every second is my work. But this gamer really didn't need a third pass, especially because there's an actual copyeditor waiting to review it. I hit my submit button and spin to face Rachel, eager for whatever kind of professional distraction she might provide. "I'm all yours."

Rachel motions for me to follow her, and we walk past the locker room, where I can hear the team celebrating their upset win against the Packers, past the coaches' offices, into a small conference room.

Sitting at the table are Judy from the Cougars' PR team and Lynn, their head of marketing. Standing off to the side are two men I don't recognize. Rachel closes the door behind us and takes a seat next to Judy and Lynn, then gestures to the chair across from them. I pull out my phone to start recording, and Judy shakes her head sharply. "Everything we're going to discuss in this room is off the record, for now."

I nod, tuck my phone away in my bag, and take the seat. No one speaks as I settle in. I've never been in a meeting with this tenor, and I can tell by the protocol that it's something big; I'm giddy with excitement.

"A member of our team has decided to come out of the closet as gay, publicly," Judy says, "and we'd like for you to be the journalist we work with on this story."

"We loved the piece you did on queer coaches with Rachel, and your reporting on the sports bars too. And of course, all of your coverage from the WNBA earlier this season," Lynn adds.

"It's one of our younger players, an active player, who is performing very well." Rachel gives me an almost-smile, something like pride. "So this isn't like a come-out-and-then-retire situation. This is a promising player at the start of his career."

"And we think you're the perfect fit, if you're interested," Lynn jumps in.

"I'm interested!" I respond a little too loudly and a little too quickly, but I also don't care if I'm making it obvious how much of a dream it would be to get to write this piece. I clear my throat and say in a much more measured tone, "I'm honored and I'm thrilled that you thought of me."

I clench my fists in my lap, trying to clear my head of any thoughts that aren't the interview that I'm about to be thrust into with no prep, no docs of notes. *They chose you for this because you've been preparing your whole life*, I tell myself and try to believe it.

Rachel steps out of the room to get the player, and I can't help trying to guess who it's going to be. Perhaps some second-stringer, a handsome white boy whose parents have an "Everyone is welcome here" sign on their lawn. Or, there's the powerhouse placekicker, who has a big social media following, paints his fingernails black, and makes videos of himself doing every dance that trends on TikTok.

I snap out of my speculative reverie to introduce myself to the strangers who have now joined us at the table. Though I don't recognize their faces, I do recognize their names: a sports agent and a publicist, presumably the personal reps for the player I'm about to be interviewing.

Rachel comes back into the room, and right behind her is the stoic rookie QB Kyland Green.

I try not to react, but he must see something on my face.

"Holy shit, right?" He laughs.

Since nothing is on the record right now, I ditch my filter. "Holy fucking shit, indeed."

Kyland chuckles as my whirring mind tries to process the gravity of the moment. There has been exactly one out, active football player—ever. And he wasn't a first-round draft pick. He certainly wasn't a star quarterback in his debut season who spent his first five games leading the team to decisive victories. Kyland Green coming out? This is going to be seismic.

"The way it's going to work is this," Judy says, speaking for the room. "On Monday, Kyland is going to post a video to his social media, and then five minutes later the *Chronicle* can publish an interview. You'll have ten minutes for a Q&A now, but our team has to vet the final quotes."

"We won't give any more comments until the pregame presser next Thursday," Kyland's personal publicist says, leaving no room for argument.

"I'll have to confirm it with my editor," I say, and when I call David on speakerphone, I count the rings, praying for him to pick up. When he does, his tone is even, but I can tell by the way he capitulates to every stipulation without negotiation that he knows this is a big fucking deal.

With the details settled, almost everyone leaves. Judy and Kyland's publicist move to chairs on either side of Kyland and take out their phones to capture the conversation. I turn on my recording app and open my computer to take notes simultaneously, mentally stringing together a strategy for the interview as quickly as I can.

"So"—I make eye contact with Kyland, ignoring the publicists flanking him—"I heard a rumor that you might be gay."

Kyland laughs, then takes me through a little bit of his personal history, starting with when he realized he was queer ("There wasn't really a time I didn't know, but there was definitely a time when I didn't wanna think about it") and a few softball questions, like his first celebrity crush ("I'm cringe as hell for this, but Matt Bomer. My mom used to watch old episodes of *White Collar* while she cooked us dinner"). We talk about the impact of Michael Sam and Carl Nassib and even—with a lot of eye-rolling—Colton Underwood.

"I'm gonna take a bit of a turn. Just follow me here, okay?" I ask.

Kyland nods.

"There is already a lot of talk about you. Conversations that I would guess you don't like very much. A lot of racism, I mean."

Kyland nods, more slowly now. "People have ideas of what a quarterback should look like, and I don't fit that description." Compared to some of the media-trained answers I've gotten on this topic in the past, this comment is practically a war cry.

"And there have never been any rumors about your sexuality."

"Nope."

"You're not doing this to get in front of a story, and it's definitely not gonna make your life any easier. In fact, it's likely to make your life off the field a lot harder. So why come out at all?"

Kyland doesn't even have to consider his answer. "Not everybody is in a position to make real change. But I'm in that position, and I want to make that change. I'm not doing this just for myself, but for all the kids who think they are too gay to play football or too Black to be a quarterback. I'm stepping into my power. That's the kind of man I want to be, on and off the field."

I get full-body chills hearing him say this. Visibility is a choice, and I'm finally acknowledging how much that matters, even for someone as under-the-radar as me.

"And on a personal level, it's actually going to make my life off the field easier, like—none of my gay friends have to walk around pretending it's nineteen-fucking-sixty," Kyland continues. "My life is good right now and I'm lucky. I don't want to spend these good, lucky years sneaking around and looking over my shoulder." He cocks his head, really looking at me. "You know this, but in the WNBA, they used to try to get all the girls to act straight, and it was the players who said, 'Nah, I'm not going to pretend anymore.' It's time for me to stop pretending too."

When the interview is officially over, as I'm double-triple-checking that my audio recording is saved, Kyland pauses in the doorway before making his exit. "I appreciate you being the one to do this. I know you'll do me right."

"You know you're going to be the first out player who was a first-round draft pick?" I say, not because he might not be aware but because I need to show him how in awe I am. "Fuck. You're going to be the first openly gay *quarterback*."

"Yeah," Kyland says, smiling big at me. "I'm a fucking trailblazer and shit."

XXII

The next morning, a few hours before Kyland's social post is scheduled to go live, I meet Casey in a part of the *LA Chronicle* offices I've avoided for years: the social media recording room. Casey grins at me so hungrily that she looks like a murderous and gleeful angler fish.

But she's not all teeth. She scheduled me immediately after an interview with Kathryn Hahn and made sure the hair and makeup team stayed long enough to do light glam for me. I ask for a swipe of black eyeliner and a slicked-back bun that reveals my undercut. When the stylist holds up her mirror, I'm everything I hope to see reflected back at me: a woman who's strong and smart, professional with an edge of sexy. And perhaps for the first time in my life, I don't feel scared or uncertain about showing that person on camera.

Casey sits me on a high stool in front of a dark gray backdrop, then fiddles with two lights and her Canon 5D for a few minutes before clipping a mic to the collar of my shirt and standing back behind the camera. She shows me where to look and then nods for me to start talking.

I explain the context of the article, rattle off Kyland's

college stats, and add some color around how phenomenally he's been performing in his rookie season.

"What does writing this story mean to you personally?" Casey asks.

I take a deep breath. "Kyland said that as someone in a position to make real change, he wants to do it both on and off the field. He's decided that's the kind of man he wants to be. I relate to that. Historically, the NFL has seemed like a space dominated by heterosexual people, but queer people have been here all along. Football is for everyone. And as a lesbian who covers the NFL, it's important for me to find those stories and shine a light on them, whether it's about Khalen Saunders's LGBTQ-friendly football camp or a player like Kyland Green deciding to share more about who he is."

I knew the question was coming and had prepped for it, but I didn't expect saying the words out loud to make me feel so powerful. And whole.

I've spent my entire professional career following David's rules for writing stories, and my rules for how I should present myself. I've been content to slip into the familiar grooves and patterns.

My entire adult life, whenever people have asked me "Why football?" I've given them a throwaway answer—something true but not revealing: "Who wouldn't love the most beautiful sport in the world?"

But the truth is that it went from interest to love affair when I was in middle school, and looking back now, I realize that's when I started to appreciate how sacred playbooks are to the sport. At each down, the team is following a template for success, and if they accomplish what is on the page, they'll achieve victory.

But what I hadn't really considered until I was ripped away from the league is what's kept me so entranced all these years: What makes each game a marvel is that it's full of surprises that aren't written into the guide. The most stunning things happen when the plays don't go as planned and the players have to follow their instincts. And the same is true for me; I am better when I know the rules but show up as myself.

"How was that?" I ask Casey. "Should we record another version?"

"No, that was perfect. Do you want to see?"

A year ago, I would've brushed off Casey's offer, avoiding any acknowledgment of myself as subject rather than author. But now I want to witness it. I slide off the stool and join Casey behind the camera, and she plays back my last answer on the tiny monitor.

"It's important for me to find those stories and shine a light on them," the miniature version of me on the screen says.

"Oh shit," I say, "I'm proud of myself."

Casey slides a hand around my waist and puts her head on my shoulder. "I'm proud of you too."

An hour later, Kyland posts his video on social media. The *LA Chronicle* publishes our interview, Casey posts the video of me on the *Chronicle* channels, and my notifications go off so hard I actually have to put my phone in a drawer. I get all the hate mail I'm anticipating. The antigay people and the shut-up-and-dribble people flood comments on everything I've posted on every channel for the past year. I get two emails that are violent and specific enough that I have to forward them to HR to ladder up to law enforcement. But if the response had been only hate, it never would've hit the fever pitch necessary to make me hide my phone. On every platform, I'm flooded by comments from gay and queer NFL fans who are crying, celebrating, and sharing their own stories.

After work, Sean FaceTimes me his gushy congratulations from outside Crypto, where fans are decked out in blue waiting to watch the second playoff game between the Liberty and the Lights. Casey buys me a martini at Bar and shows me some TikToks she's saved. In the *LA Chronicle* article, I'd included Kyland's comments about WNBA players refusing to stay in the closet, and it seems like every WNBA player I've ever interviewed—and a bunch I've never even met—has posted something about the story. I do my best to focus on what a win that is for the article and not let the pain of Natalie's proximity to it distract me from the emotional victory lap I'm trying to take.

After Casey does what she calls her "press recap," I am bubbling over with the weirdest, headiest pride I've ever felt. She flicks back to the *LA Chronicle*'s account and the interview with me. I glance at the comments and smile at one from Weesie: "LET'S FUCKING GOOOOOO." Just above that I see highlights of who's liked the video, and Natalie Czapski's handle is right there. Seeing her name is like a caress and a slap from the same hand.

On the TV above my head, the Lights-Liberty matchup starts. Sean had let me know that Natalie passed concussion protocols this morning, which means her injury wasn't even bad enough to keep her out of a single game. On the screen, she backs up against Jonquel Jones on the Liberty, stepping, faking, managing to sink a tough two-pointer.

"Do you want to change the channel?" Casey asks, gently.

I shake my head. "I want to watch. Are you emotionally capable of comforting me if I cry?"

Casey wrinkles her nose. "I regret the day Sean got an assignment that means I'm forced to be your shoulder to cry on. I don't know how!"

"I'll talk you through it," I say.

I try to let myself experience the game as a fan, and even though I can't take my eyes off Natalie or stop thinking about her, I don't cry. She's playing too fucking well for me to land anywhere close to sad. She picks Sabrina Ionescu's pocket in transition and hits an easy layup to tie the game just before halftime. The announcer quips, *"CZ is so deep in her bag, she found some loose Tic Tacs."*

In the second half, Natalie plays like crazy, shooting 74 percent from the field and getting to the line over and over again. She runs flawless screens for Jada Jackson, who sinks shot after shot, scoring an insane thirty-seven points. Against all the odds, they eke out a win against the Liberty, forcing a third game in the series.

The sideline reporter pulls Natalie for a postgame interview as the rest of the Lights players jump and scream.

"That was just an incredible performance, Nat. How did you play on such a high level today?"

Natalie grins so bright to the camera I feel like we might all go blind. "I was playing inspired."

The next morning I wake up in a haze of euphoria tempered by the dull throb that surfaces every time the reality of my heartbreak sets in. I roll over and check my phone, prepared to distract myself by contending with some of the digital overwhelm I've been avoiding. At the top of my notifications is a text message: a screenshot of a ticket for game three in the friends and family section and the message "Please?" If I was playing by my rules I would shut this down, maybe even ignore it. But I'm not anymore.

XXIII

When I walk into the arena, the team is still warming up, practicing free throws. The social media crew is circling the players, filming content. The most ardent fans are waiting by the tunnel entrance to beg for signatures when the players pass by, Lights merch and Sharpies clutched in their hands.

As I make my way to the friends and family section, I spot Romy and Jay in their usual spot behind the players' bench. Instead of taking the seat farthest away, I slide into the one next to Romy with a "This seat taken?"

"Look who finally decided to join us." She's as pointed as ever.

"Good to see you," Jay says, grinning for the both of them.

"Good to see you two."

As warm-ups end, Natalie glances to where I usually sit, looking for me. I watch her eyes scan, trying to read her body language and facial expression. Eventually, she spots me. Her smile takes over her face like she can't help it. I don't want to make myself vulnerable by grinning back, but I also can't help the way my lips curve, just a little. Her smile is too infectious and the hope inside me is too big. She shouts, "Meet me after the game?" I nod, big enough for her to see.

And then it begins, and the moment is the same as it always is. Anticipation, suspense, possibility. The excited chatter of fans, the salty smells of hot dogs and popcorn, the boom of the announcer's voice as he names the starting lineup. Any player can become a hero; any team can win. But just because anything can happen, that doesn't mean anything will. Possibility is just the start—you have to leap for it. To make a shot, you have to risk missing.

The Hollywood Lights are a tenacious, dynamic, speedy young team that ooze potential every time they take the court, but the New York Liberty are a dynasty, with some of the best players in the league at the peak of their game. The Liberty take the lead early and refuse to give it up. Natalie plays well, and the Lights fight and fight and fight during every possession, but the Liberty just have it today.

One minute before the end of the last quarter, the Liberty are up by fifteen. The Lights will surely lose—there's no way around it. I notice someone break away from the cluster of publicists waiting to coordinate the postgame interviews. Ashley navigates through our section to crouch next to my seat and ask if I wouldn't mind following her to the press room.

As a sports fan, I generally consider it sacrilege to leave before gameplay ends, especially if your team is down. You stay and support until the final buzzer calls. But the flutter of hope that's lived in my stomach since Natalie texted me the tickets is stronger than my sense of decorum, and I follow Ashley.

She leads me through hallways I'm familiar with and then some that I'm not. I realize these are places that players and staff get to go that journalists don't when she stops me outside of a door that I've never seen before but says "Media Room" on the placard: the door the players use on their path between the locker room and the presser.

"Do you mind waiting out here?" Ashley asks. She's looking distractedly at her phone, but there's something in her tone, not to mention her actions, indicating that she's Natalie's compatriot in some plan. I want to hope it's something good. I flash back to Natalie's big smile, her text that just said "Please?"—begging me for something. But I also think of all her dismissals and the coldness when she turned away from me.

"Sure," I say, as mildly as I can manage, and Ashley pulls open the door to the press room. It snicks closed behind her, and I'm by myself in the hallway, alone with my racing thoughts and thumping heart.

I hear footsteps and voices. A small group rounds the far corner: the Lights' coach with his head buried in a stapled packet of game stats, another publicist I recognize, and Jada and Olivia, despondently chatting like they'd rather talk than not talk in the aftermath of a big, bad loss. Behind them is Natalie.

They start walking past me with barely a glance, ready to file into the press room and get things over with. I wonder if Natalie is going to follow them. I don't understand why I'm here. Every muscle in my body is tense, ready to collapse if she just passes me by.

Natalie stops and says low to the group, "Give me just a sec."

And then we're alone in the hallway. I cross my arms like that will protect me from whatever this is. Natalie leans against the cement block wall. For a second, she doesn't look at me, avoidant. Then her eyes meet mine, suddenly intense, like she turned on a switch.

"I fucked up," she says, too loud for the empty hallway.

"Yeah, I mean . . ." I try to think clearly, remember what I need to express to her, but she starts talking again.

"I really fucked up, I know I really fucked up, and honestly I know I've fucked up in the past, but I've never really had to clean up after any of my messes, at least none of my emotional ones, but I have to do something. I'm trying to do something. I'm—"

I've never heard Natalie ramble before. As far as I know, "Natty Ice, the Smooth Operator" has never rambled in her whole entire life. Until she rambled for me.

I squeeze my eyes shut, as if that could hold back my feelings, keep them from crashing over me like a wave.

Natalie sighs. "I think I need to see a therapist."

My eyes fly open as a burst of laughter escapes my mouth. It's not enough, not yet, but it does mean I can ask for more, ask for what I need.

"I need you to actually say 'I'm sorry,'" I respond.

"Oh shit, yeah, fuck, I didn't say I'm sorry."

"Nope, you did not." I force myself not to hide from her. "You still haven't."

"Felix, I'm so sorry I hurt you. You didn't deserve it." She laughs. "I mean—fuck, of course you didn't deserve it. I want a chance to make it right again."

I feel too close to her, and too far away. And like I want to give her everything and ask for more but I'm so scared to do both.

Then the door swings open and Ashley steps into the frame, blocking our view from the reporters gathered inside. She makes an apologetic face. "Natalie, we really need you to step inside," she says.

Natalie looks at her, then looks at me.

"Go," I say. "We can talk more later."

Natalie nods, then slips into the room, and I expect the door to close between us, but Ashley beckons me to follow, then points toward the back of the room.

Natalie settles into her seat at the table facing the press, glancing at the stat sheet to reorient herself and adjusting the microphone in front of her. Olivia, on her left, covers her mic and whispers something to Natalie.

"All good," Natalie says.

I lean against the rear wall, my eyes mostly on Natalie. I note that the crowd is bigger and less local than usual, with beat reporters from the New York papers and WNBA and basketball generalists from all over the country covering the playoffs. A few of them clock me—no one without a press badge shows up in the media room—but don't seem to spare me much brain space.

Sean's sitting in the back row, and he turns around in his seat and says, "Good luck . . . with whatever this is," before turning back to his laptop.

The publicists kick off the press conference, and the tone starts out subdued, respectful of the loss.

Then, a reporter I've never seen in a Lights presser before asks in a snide voice if Natalie thinks the Lights would've won game one if she'd been on the court the full game. It's an awful question. Every professional athlete has been brought up since childhood to think that anytime they can't be there for the team, they've let everyone down and their absence has caused a loss. It's not cockiness so much as a delusion shared by all players.

"I don't know." Natalie spits the same venom at him she did at me my first day. "Do *you* think my team would've won if I'd played through a grade-two concussion?"

At last, the publicists call for final questions, and Natalie leans into the mic, "I actually have a question to ask." The PR in charge of calling on reporters looks uncertain what to do. Natalie barrels on. "I was wondering if Jennifer Felix from the *LA Chronicle* wanted to ask anything."

The room doesn't know how to interpret it, especially given Sean's presence in the room, but there's a hum of whispers. Enough people here know I'm not supposed to be covering the game. Eyes land on me, and for a moment, I'm all panic. But then the spotlight on me feels strangely warm. And when I see Natalie's smile and the quirk of her eyebrow, I realize that I know my line: The same thing I asked her the first time I was in this room.

"How's your injury recovery going?" My heart is racing from the attention of her gaze.

"Working on it. Been trying to remind myself that this is just a game—basketball isn't my *wife*," she smirks.

I laugh a little, uncharacteristically gleeful but unable to resist her charm.

Then she asks, "How is *your* injury recovery going?"

The room goes still. I can feel gazes flicking between us, feel the heat of their confusion scraping against my skin.

I look at Natalie and only Natalie, letting the rest of it fall away. Maybe this is what it feels like to be a player at an away game, blocking out the boos to sink a free throw. To stand up even when your body—your heart—is still aching.

I've spent so long trying to describe the buzz of sports to other people. But now I realize: The real story is in the choice to keep playing.

Natalie asked me how I was healing, knowing exactly what she broke.

"Poised for a comeback," I say.

Keep cheering for Felix and Natalie: Read the book's epilogue to see where these two go from here, and snag your own Hollywood Lights fan gear while you're at it. Just scan below or visit 831stories.com/rootinginterest.

More novellas like this one are waiting for you at 831stories.com, where we celebrate romantic fiction in all its forms. You can also dive into bonus content, products, events, and fan fiction and join our membership program to receive new releases early, get discounts across the site, and access all sorts of exclusive perks.

ACKNOWLEDGMENTS

Claire and Erica, thank you for championing this book from start to finish. You treat your authors and their books with such care, creativity, and attention—you've ruined me for all future publishing endeavors. It's also thanks to you that Natalie Czapski has a fully developed frontal lobe. Thank you to my copyeditors for saving me from *it's* versus *its*–related embarrassment.

Thank you to Georgia Clark for helping me unlock Felix's emotional arc, and thank you to Sanjana Basker for reminding me that Felix could feel things in other places than "the space beneath her ribs."

Thank you to Zan Romanoff. This novel wouldn't exist without you. But also, thank you for our years of friendship and writing camaraderie. I will always be a big fan.

Thank you to the Shitty First Drafts writing group for all of your feedback, encouragement, and support. I can't believe how lucky I am to have you all as my early readers.

Thank you to Aubrey Bellamy, Alice Royer, Ed Blair, Erika Paget, Anna Dorn, Jett Allen, Sydney Kim, and

Kelsey Ford for letting me bounce ideas off of you, for recommending me books, for listening to my long-winded plot explanations. Thank you to Nikki Ulrich and Erica Tully for the decades together.

Thank you to Ramou Sarr for all the WNBA talk and the Paige memes. Basketball is fun!! Thank you to Sarah Enni for teaching me everything I know about the NFL and helping me fan the flame of my sports enthusiasm. Thank you to everyone who went to a WNBA game with me and let me point out who on the teams were dating each other.

Thank you to all my friends for always asking me how the book was going and for being equally supportive when it was going well and when I was having a mental breakdown about it.

Thank you to the dearly departed Greyhound Bar & Grill in Glendale, where I wrote at least 50 percent of this novel. It turns out, my new love of watching the WNBA was a perfect fit with my old love of going to the bar. Thank you to all the bartenders who took such good care of me there, especially Tony.

Thank you to Dorland Mountain Arts Colony for hosting me while I conceptualized this novel. Thank you to Edan Lepucki, Darcy Vebber, and Kristen Daniels, who cooked me dinner and talked me through the rough patches of the outline.

Thank you to my parents, my siblings, and Percie. My love for you is the only love so big I can't put it into words.

ABOUT THE AUTHOR

Cat DiSabato's first novel, *The Ghost Network*, was deemed "a smart and thorny debut" by *The New York Times*, and her second, *U Up?*, was named a 2021 *NYT* Best Mystery. She lives in Los Angeles, and her rooting interest is the Los Angeles Sparks.

ALSO FROM 831 STORIES

Big Fan by Alexandra Romanoff
A high-profile scandal derailed Maya's DC career, and she's eager to fly under the radar—that is, until her former boy-band crush reaches out with a job offer.

Hardly Strangers by A.C. Robinson
One night with a rock star could upend Shera's best-laid plans, revealing how a chance encounter can rewrite a story—and change everything.

Comedic Timing by Upasna Barath
Naina is seeking a fresh start in NYC after breaking up with her girlfriend, but when she meets someone at a party, he's so offtype that her attraction to him fuels an identity crisis.

Set Piece by Lana Schwartz
When a breakout BBC star gets swarmed by fans during a night out, it's a no-nonsense bartender, CJ, who rescues him—and warms them both up for an after-hours hookup.

Square Waves by Alexandra Romanoff
The first spin-off in the *Big Fan* series, an enemies-to-lovers romance in which tabloid fodder mixes with a long-brewing rivalry as Cassidy contends with her high-school nemesis.

Exit Lane by Erika Veurink

A postcollege cross-country road trip sparks *something* between Marin and Teddy—though it's not quite clear what. Over the next eight years, they have fated encounters on multiple continents.

Grape Juice by Eliza Dumais

When Alice lands in France for a wine harvest, she's disenchanted with her life. But she soon finds something she's missing in the vineyard owner's nephew Henri, who's just as lost as she is.

831 STORIES BOOK CREDITS

So many people were involved in bringing this book to life. Many of their names are included here, but there would be no HEA without the passionate work of booksellers and librarians and the enthusiasm of readers. And as we all know, romance readers are the best readers.

831 Stories

Erica Cerulo, Marie Joh, Catherine Krenzer, Claire Mazur, Elaine Orihuela, Angela Vang

Authors Equity

Andrea Bachofen, Rose Edwards, Carly Gorga, Sarah Christensen Fu, Deb Lewis, Madeline McIntosh, Nina von Moltke, Diana Simmons, Erin Vandeveer, Don Weisberg, Craig Young

C47 Design

Phil Chang, Haneu Kang, Jamin Lee, Naomi Otsu, Sunny Park

Editing

Sanjana Basker, Georgia Clark

Marketing, Events, and Publicity

Emma Benshoff, Tara Larsen, Ashleigh Magee, Kaitlin Phillips, Riley Vaske, Kristin White

Production

Sam Martin, Scribe Inc.

Keep reading for a taste of

Comedic Timing

by Upasna Barath

from 831 Stories

I

Armed with a bottle of red wine, I approach a stranger's home seeking a clean slate. No one at this party knows me. No one has an opinion on my breakup, barely a month old. No one needs to choose sides. I left Chicago, and I live in New York now—even if it's only been two days.

I arrive at a brownstone in Bed-Stuy. I try the buzzer and wait for five minutes, chilly in the cool air of a September evening. A breeze brushes against me, raising the hairs on my exposed limbs. I should have worn layers. I double-check my hair with my phone camera before calling someone named Christian, who I'd been put in touch with via text. He appears and prances down the steps, his hair even blonder than in his photos on social media. He greets me with a bear hug.

"Naina," he says into my shoulder, as if we're childhood friends who haven't seen each other in years. "So good to meet you."

"Nice to meet you too," I respond, laughing at his easygoing familiarity, the yeasty smell of beer on his breath. "Jordan says hi. I brought wine."

"Pshhh, you didn't have to," he says, taking the bottle. "Come on inside."

The distant hum of traffic gives way to the typical sound of some party, somewhere: voices and music, muffled and thumping above the creaky staircase Christian gestures for me to climb.

We approach the apartment door, and he swings it open to reveal a duplex space. Bodies are bathed in moody, atmospheric lighting. My chest pulses with bass. I have never been inside such a spacious, and likely expensive, apartment. There's an ultramodern, bulbous-looking couch dominating the living room and a hand-knotted rug—the kind my mother would have fawned over—at its center. There are a half dozen people sitting on the ground, holding red wine in an assortment of mismatched glassware.

Compared to most of the other guests, my outfit feels both too formal and yet insufficient: a little black dress. Everyone's looks are curated with the right mix of outdated (presumably thrifted) pieces—scarves, wide-leg pants, sparkly tops—and newer ones, evidence of an understanding, or at least an acceptance, of the importance of fashion. These are the kind of people who sit on nice furniture while sipping wine out of repurposed jars.

People flow in and out from the balcony. Cigarette smoke floats over their heads and into the apartment. I suddenly feel very small, or perhaps just very young, momentarily regressing to a meekness I haven't felt since I graduated college three years ago.

Christian smiles at me assuredly.

"I live here with two roommates," he explains. "Rana and my friend David, who you missed singing 'Happy Birthday' to."

"Oh no," I respond. "I love singing 'Happy Birthday' to strangers."

"I'll introduce you when I find him," Christian says. "Want some cake?"

In the kitchen, Christian and I squeeze past a group of friends wheezing with laughter. Christian was right—the wine was unnecessary. The kitchen counter is chock-full of bottles and empty beer cans indistinguishable from half-drunk ones.

He opens mine anyway. "Sorry, don't know where all the glasses are," he says, rifling through cabinets. From the counter, I pick up a red Solo cup with the name "Margot" written on it in black Sharpie. "Don't worry, Margot left me hers," I say. Christian snorts, grabbing the cup to rinse it before serving me a generous pour.

"Your apartment is very cool," I say.

"Thanks," he says. "It's changed a lot. We've been living here for seven years, almost."

"Whoa," I respond. "That's commitment."

"In one area of my life," he says, shrugging.

Christian digs a vape out from his pocket—hot pink, like some kind of toy—and offers me a hit. I take it and inhale, even though I don't really vape, and I know it's terrible for you.

"Trying to quit," he says, as if reading my mind.

"Remind me how you know Jordan?" I ask, referring to my best friend who introduced us and promised that we'd get along.

"I met him at a mutual friend's comedy show. I *hooked up* with said mutual friend," Christian adds with a drop of pride, as if announcing he'd won an award. "And I debriefed with him. I didn't know who else to talk to about it. Been pals ever since."

"That's sweet. I love my morning-after debriefs with Jordan," I respond, hoping to conceal the very real sadness I feel from missing my friend. Our postmortems would feel different now with eight hundred miles between us.

"How do you know Jordan?"

"College," I reply.

"Are you in comedy too?"

"No. I could never," I reply. I don't mean for this to come off as derogatory, so I add, "But I respect it. And most of my friends are comedians."

Christian squints cynically at my comment and continues: "Has anyone ever told you that you shouldn't be friends with comedians?" He laughs, grabbing a bottle of beer from the fridge. He digs a set of keys from his pocket, looking down to find what he needs, and pops the cap swiftly.

"Mostly that I shouldn't date them," I say. "But I really do laugh more because of Jordan. I'm a writer, to answer your next question."

"That's cool. Is that what you do for money?" He sips his beer as if testing it, then tilts the bottle back for more.

I try not to look crestfallen at this involuntary reminder

of my reality. I clear my throat. "For money I work in marketing."

"Ah." Christian nods.

"One day, you know, I hope to write for money."

"Totally. So, what do you write?"

I gulp my wine. I haven't had to talk about this yet in this new city. I don't know how it will feel. "Mostly satirical essays. Commentary on internet culture." I turn the question back to him. "So what do you do for money?"

"I work as a software engineer," he says, grimacing. "But I tell people I'm a comedian because that's what I am. I used to be in an improv group in college. That's how I met my roommates." He tilts the bottle back again, filling his cheeks with the liquid before swallowing.

"What do they do?"

"David's a filmmaker," Christian explains. "Well, I mean, for money, he's a video editor. My other roommate, Rana, is a social worker."

A woman enters the kitchen and places her hand on the back of Christian's neck. "Speak of the devil," Christian says. Without addressing me, Rana asks for his vape, securing it before swiftly exiting the room.

"Please know that outside of this context, I'm not inhaling from an adult pacifier every five minutes," Christian says. "I just really wanted it for the party."

"What's going on there?" I ask Christian, gesturing toward the strange, flirtatious dynamic between him and his roommate.

"Oh no. Rana has a boyfriend," he says. "She's just

really affectionate when she's drunk. And on Molly. She's on Molly."

"Ah."

"We've hooked up before, but no—just friends. And roommates."

"Oh, the old lovers-to-friends-to-roommates pipeline," I say.

"What about you? You single?"

I steady myself to respond neutrally. "I just broke up with my girlfriend. Incidentally, she's also a software engineer."

"How boring," he says, grinning and nudging me with his elbow. We already have an in-joke.

"But I applied for a job here, just to see if I'd get it. I did, so I moved. I just wanted a fresh start. I've been here for a few days now."

"Well, are you okay? Since the breakup?"

"Not really. But I will be soon, don't worry."

"Well, yeah. I can tell you're the dumper, not the dumpee." He gulps more beer and swallows a burp.

I consider clarifying that even though I did the breaking up, I don't feel like I came out on top. All my and Sofia's mutual friends are checking in on her, while I have been turned into the villain. I only have Jordan to confide in. Sofia is clearly the more sympathetic person in this situation. Defending myself would do nothing to change that.

I tell Christian to go play host—it's not his responsibility to entertain me—and after my third and decidedly last cup of wine, I run into the Margot who I suspect belongs to the cup I commandeered. She drunkenly introduces herself by pointing at it with her mouth open. "You're a Margot?" she asks, shouting over the music, pushing a wisp of blond hair away from her face.

"Whoa. Freaky," I say. "We look alike too."

She blinks, then bursts into laughter.

"No, not a Margot. I'm Naina," I say. "I stole your cup."

"I thought you were for real!" she exclaims. "I'm pathologically gullible."

We find ourselves on the balcony with Margot's friend, who sports a mullet, discussing dating deal-breakers: Mullet says he could never date someone who can't handle spicy food. Margot tells him to get his priorities straight. Christian joins, passing a joint, and when it makes its way to me, I take a baby hit.

"Want to come upstairs?" Christian asks me, his head cocked to the side. Margot raises her eyebrows and looks away, as if to pretend she can't hear us. "The drug room," Mullet states ominously, his voice dropping an octave. I ask if they're joining. Margot shakes her head, evading eye contact with Christian.

Mullet waves goodbye, like a princess. "'Twas a pleasure," he sings.

"Margot's a stand-up comic, but she's not that funny," Christian whispers to me as we climb the stairs.

I roll my eyes. "You sound jealous," I say, poking him. "Comedians are so competitive. What's the story there?"

"Margot is an old friend. It's not my business to share, but Margot and David—my other roommate?—were together for two years. We were all friends, then they started dating, and it got messy."

"This is why I don't get dating apps," I say. "Why download them to meet up with a stranger when you can just corrupt the dynamics of your friend group?"

When we make it to the upstairs room, I'm stoned, and my body feels the tug of the queen-size bed. I climb atop it with a few strangers.

"How long were you together?" Christian asks, squeezing himself in next to me. "You and your girlfriend?"

"We met when I was nineteen," I say. "She's five years older."

"How many people have you dated?"

"That was my only relationship ever."

"Wow," Christian says, weirdly in awe.

He looks at a text message on his phone. I wonder if I'm boring him. "Be right back, duty calls," he says. When he leaves, I turn my attention to a stack of books sitting on top of a patched-up fireplace, a mix of self-help and American classics. Next to me, a woman snorts a line of something off a small tray. We make eye contact as she gently rubs her nose.

"Hey," she says.

"Hi. Oh, I like your eyeshadow. Blue. Nice." *Awkward.*

She dabs at her nostrils with her ring finger. "Thanks, girl. Want some?"

"Coke?" I ask. She nods.

"Oh," I respond, weirdly embarrassed. I am tempted to snort a line despite never having snorted anything. I am suspicious of my urge to let loose, wondering if it is a good or bad thing. I shake my head, forcing myself not to look away as her blotting turns to vehement wiping.

The door swings open with sitcom flair, drawing everyone's attention. A tall man steps in, and they all slowly break into "Happy Birthday." "It ended two hours ago," he replies as he gestures for calm, his arms moving in gentle, measured arcs. "I'm here to use my bathroom, don't mind me." David, Christian's roommate. He smiles at everyone with a quiet magnetism, the kind that makes a person instantly likable without effort. My eyes scan him, catching on the thick hair that curls around his ears, his sharp jaw, the strain of his shoulders against the cotton of his shirt. I assume he's used to being the most attractive person in the room by default.

"Want some?" the cocaine girl asks him. He grimaces, revealing a few crooked bottom teeth. "Did you test that?" he asks. She shrugs.

"Don't shrug at me!" David teases. "I'm not judging you. Just be safe. We have test strips in the kitchen drawer downstairs, for future reference."

"So you don't want any?" she asks him. David shakes his head.

"Aw come on. You used to be fun," she replies.

"Are you peer pressuring me?" he jokes. She shrugs again. I can't tell if they're flirting, but something about their interaction makes me uncomfortable enough to want to interrupt.

"He's right," I chime in. "Why not just test it?"

David's eyes find mine, and I meet his gaze, noticing a boyish sincerity etched in his expression. He suddenly turns self-conscious, brushing something off his shirt, white and crisp like he ironed it. His bicep flexes subtly.

"See?" he says, gesturing to me with his thumb. "You hear her?" The woman rolls her eyes at us and leaves the room, either to get the strips or to escape the conversation.

David turns to me, smiling and squinting. His eyes crinkle mischievously. "Can you believe that?" he asks. "So cavalier."

"I know, right?" I reply, laughing.

"I haven't seen you before, have I?" he asks, his gaze shifting over me.

"No, you haven't," I reply. "Unless you're mistaking me for some other brown woman!" I poke him in his shoulder playfully, but it lands flat. *What made me say that?*

He pulls his chin in. "Why would I do that? I'm brown."

"I see that. What kind of brown are you?" I ask, crossing my arms. *Oh, good, I am making it worse.*

He lets out a single laugh, *ha*. "That's pretty racist, you know."

I fake a scoff, relieved to have him playing along. "Not racist."

"What's your name?" he asks.

"Naina," I say as I hold out my hand. "Thanks for having me. Christian invited me."

He takes my hand, and we exchange what is not so much of a handshake as a brief handhold. It's less a greeting and more an excuse to touch the other person. We might both be guilty of making it that way. I feel his calluses press against my palm. He finally releases his grip.

"I'm David."

"Happy birthday," I tell him. My brain is on a lag, I realize. My wrist is still extended in his direction. I force my hand down, hoping my mind will catch up. "How old are we?"

"Thirty-two."

"You don't look a day over twenty-seven," I reply. David snorts.

"Thanks. Christian didn't mention he was seeing anyone," he says.

"Um, no, we're not—I just got out of a breakup. And then I moved here. From Chicago." I've repeated a variation of this explanation so many times tonight. This time it comes out in a string of breathless words. *Why am I desperate to let him know I am single and definitely not dating Christian?*

"So, you ran away," he says, curling his lip teasingly. In a sense, he's correct, but I won't tell him that.

"Actually, I got a job here."

"Congrats. That's great news. Except maybe not so much for your ex-boyfriend."

"Ex-girlfriend."

David pulls his chin in again, this time out of surprise. "Huh."

"What?"

"I wouldn't have guessed," he responds with a shrug. I'm confused, not sure what to make of this statement. *He wouldn't have guessed what?* He looks me up and down quickly, as if trying to solve something. I turn self-conscious, feeling trapped in the fucking LBD. The dress accentuates my femmeness, my D-cup breasts, the curve of my waist that my mother deemed part of my "lovely figure." It suddenly feels too short, this dress that previously sat untouched at the back of my closet for years. Tonight, however, it had made its way into a first impression by virtue of being one of the least rumpled things to emerge from my moving boxes.

To this man, me being queer is a surprise because of the way I look. Blood rushes to my face, igniting a silent fury.

His face turns concerned. "What?"

"Do you usually just go around making assumptions about people's sexuality?" I ask tersely.

The energy between us twists. He covers his face. His nails are short, as if bitten.

"I'm . . . very sorry. That's not what I—that was stupid," he says through nervous laughter. "I didn't mean it that way; I wasn't thinking."

I blink at him, wondering what he could have meant other than *You don't look queer to me.*

I cross my arms, and he cups my elbows, his face softening as mine hardens. "Can we start over?" he asks, his voice quieter. "But I *really* need to pee, so let me do that first. Don't go anywhere."

He disappears into the bathroom. The coke girl returns, test strips in hand, waving them at me as if to say *See?!* I want to wait for David, at least to hear his version of "starting over," but wearing this outfit, meeting these people, and being out in this world has turned from novel to unbearable. I crave the comfort of being alone, with myself: of peeling the dress off my body, scrubbing the city off my face, and crawling under my duvet, naked.

I walk downstairs and gently push myself through a group of people dancing to a Mischief song I loved in high school. I hold my breath against a wicked mix of stale cigarettes and strong perfume. I pause to look for Christian, to say goodbye, but I give up after one scan of the crowd.

Determined to escape, I shove open the apartment door and jog down the stairs of the building, landing on the balls of my feet. I step into the cool air of the night, mood lighting now swapped for the dim fluorescence of streetlamps.

I fidget with the hem of my dress, as if stretching it down will somehow make it grow longer. In all my time living in Chicago, I never did drugs, despite Jordan's penchant for microdosing shrooms at birthday parties. I rarely drank more than I could handle. But I also wasn't comfortable meeting new people, and I didn't always speak my mind. Substances aside—my Irish exit aside—I had fun tonight. I surprised myself.

I could see my life in New York as an opportunity to do something I'd never done before: It was an opportunity to grow. As I wait for a car to take me home, I give myself permission to try.